The Rich Shall Inherit

DA Lacey was born into a large family, being the youngest, she had three sisters and six brothers. She lives in Surrey with her husband. They have four children and nine grandchildren. As a child Dorothy always had a book in her hand, so it seemed a natural progression to write in later life.

The Rich Shall Inherit

D A Lacey

The Rich Shall Inherit

Olympia Publishers

www.olympiapublishers.com
OLYMPIA PAPERBACK EDITION

A CIP catalogue record for this title is
available from the British Library.

This is a work of fiction.
Names, characters, places and incidents originate from the writer's
imagination. Any resemblance to actual persons, living or dead, is
purely coincidental.

ISBN: 978-1-84897-068-7

First Published in 2010

Olympia Publishers part of Ashwell Publishing Ltd
60 Cannon Street
London
EC4N 6NP
Printed in Great Britain

To Peter,
my husband and my best friend

Prologue

The accident had only just happened. The two riders reined in their horses and the man went to dismount. The young woman moved her horse alongside, making it impossible for her companion to do so. Someone had covered the body with a blanket but a mass of vibrant red-gold hair was still visible, splayed over the hard white ground making a vivid contrast to the frost covering the spiky grass. The man on the horse stared down at the bright splash of colour and a feeling of immense sadness came over him. He felt as if he had suffered a great loss and he didn't know why. His head started to ache again and he knew it would soon develop into the blinding agony that would drag him down once again into a world of pain and confusion. He seemed unable to tear his eyes away from the scene before him. It was as if he were hypnotised. At the back of his mind, something was screaming out to him, something he knew was vital, if only he could remember.

The young woman glanced quickly at the man staring down at the thick tresses of hair. Even in death, it was beautiful, still looking as if it were glowing with life She leaned over and taking the reins of the other horse, led them both away. It wasn't an act of kindness that had made her do this, nor was it to spare the young man from a distressing sight; it was because she was afraid that if she had stayed a minute longer she would have given herself away.

Her instinct had been to leap from her horse, tear aside the blanket and gaze at that face for the very last time. That face had been the cause of many a sleepless night for her. She had known who it was the instant she had seen that unmistakeable hair. How she had hated that hair. It was a hatred born of envy. For years, she had loved this man by her side. Loved him with a passion that was almost impossible to bear. Things would have worked out if this woman hadn't entered their lives.

There was no pity in her heart for the loss of a young life. She had wanted things to be as they once were. Well it looked like things would get back to normal now. Back to how they were before that common little shop girl had ruined everything.

A smile came to her lips as the thought of what would happen now if she had her way.

Tim would never regain his memory and the world was at her feet again.

Chapter One

Jenny took a quick look in the mirror to make sure her hair had stayed put, she wasn't used to wearing it up but she could hardly start a new job with her hair flying all over the place.

She cast a quick glance over herself and satisfied that she looked presentable pulled on her coat.

Running down the stairs she called out to her younger brother Ben, "I'm off now Ben, see you tonight and don't forget to look for a job today. No excuses mind."

Ben was five years younger than Jenny, he was seventeen and had been spoilt most of his life.

He scowled at Jenny but decided not to argue with her today.

"Wish me luck then," she said.

Ben put his arm on her shoulder. "You won't need luck sis," he said. "Anyway you look great."

Jenny looked into his eyes, which were the exact colour of her own, a striking green. His hair was the same sandy colour as their father's had been while hers was the colour of their mother's, a beautiful deep red-gold. It was thick and wavy, the envy of many.

All at once, she felt lonely and afraid again. She pulled Ben into her arms and gave him a hug.

"See you later kiddo," she said and went out.

On her way to the bus stop, she thought over the past few months. It had been difficult for them but at last, things were looking up.

Their parents had both been killed in a train accident last year.

There was no money, just enough from an insurance policy to pay for the funerals, the house they lived in went with their father's job so three months after they buried their parents they were homeless. Jenny had a small amount of savings and so was just about able to pay the deposit on the rent of a modest two-bedroom house. She had been lucky to have found a job that was quite near their home, in a large department store. She was worried about her brother. Their mother had always spoiled him and now Jenny was having a hard time trying to keep him in order. After the death of their parents, Ben had gone off the rails and had been in trouble with the police. He was now on probation. Jenny worried about the company he was keeping, especially a young man by the name of Tony and Tony's girlfriend Liz. Tony was three years older than Ben. He was tall and thin with dark eyes and hair. He thought he was irresistible to women. His girlfriend, a punk rocker, adored him. Jenny had on more than one occasion come very close to slapping his face because Tony had a way of standing very close to her and touching her, which made her flesh creep.

Tony didn't have a job but he always seemed to have plenty of money, which was another worry for Jenny. Ben was very easily led and Jenny had tried to discourage his friendship with Tony but Ben seemed fascinated by him. She also worried about the late hours Ben had been keeping, Jenny felt there was nothing in her life at the moment except worry. Arriving at the bus stop she was relieved to see there weren't too many people waiting. A young woman of about her age gave her a big smile and wished her good morning. The bus came into view and soon Jenny was on board. Sinking into her seat she gave a sigh of relief.

In no time at all she was getting off the bus and she was able to see Knights department store. She felt a bit apprehensive as she stood outside for a few minutes looking up at it. She hadn't realised it was so big. Would she like it she wondered. Mentally telling herself to get on with it she straightened her shoulders and walked through the door, taking the first step into her future. A future filled with happiness and heartache.

******

Jenny stroked the sumptuous velvet of a beautiful evening gown as she put it back on the hanger. It was a beautiful jade green and she thought how well it would have suited her as she held it up to herself in the mirror. With a sigh she mentally told herself to stop dreaming. She would never be able to afford a gown like that and even if she could she never went anywhere to be able to wear it.

A small grey head popped around the door of the fitting room, it was Mrs Jenkins, Head of the Department.

"Don't you want to go home tonight Miss Woods?"

Jenny looked at her watch and was surprised to discover it was well past closing time

"How time flies when you're having fun," she said.

Mrs Jenkins gave her a friendly push towards the door. "Away you go now and don't be late in the morning."

She stood for a second watching Jenny walk away. In the past few months Jenny had become more confident in her work, she was popular with staff and customer, quite a difference from the shy girl who had started work at Knights department store last year.

Switching off the light Mrs Jenkins headed for home.

******

When Jenny walked into the staffroom she found her friend Tina waiting for her with growing impatience.

"For goodness sake get a move on Jenny. You haven't changed your mind about coming have you?"

"Not likely. I want to find out if this bloke of yours is as wonderful as you say he is."

The two girls were soon wrapped up against the cold and were on their way to the pub to meet up with Tina's fiancé and his friend.

Pushing open the door they were met with a cacophony of noise. The place was full of people and smoke.

Tina pointed to a table in an alcove.

"There he is," she cried, and made a dash for the young man who had seen them come in. He swept her up in his arms and planted a big kiss on her lips.

After he had put her down he turned to Jenny and held out his hand to her saying, "You must be Jenny, the one we have to find a bloke for."

Jenny felt herself going very red but this man had such a twinkle in his eye and such a big grin that it was impossible to be cross with him.

Tina dug him in the ribs and tried unsuccessfully to look cross with him.

"This is Bill," she said to Jenny and gave him a look that was pure adoration

"I'm delighted to make your acquaintance Miss Woods," he said, standing to attention and giving her a salute.

Tiny gave him a push. "For goodness sake behave yourself Bill and sit down."

"Let me introduce my friend to you Jenny. This is my good friend who despite looking dim has just become a fully-fledged doctor. I give you Doctor Richard Evans."

For the first time Jenny became aware of the man sitting quietly watching the exchanges going on. She found herself looking into a pair of warm brown eyes. He had a face that was not quite handsome but nevertheless there was something about him that drew Jenny at once. His hair was dark brown, falling over his eyes in its unruliness and he had the most endearing dimple in his cheek.

Jenny was embarrassed to find she was blushing again but she looked Richard full in the face.

"Congratulations," she said.

"Thank you," responded Richard. "I suppose I had better get the first round in."

"Let me give you a hand," Jenny said, "it will give these two a chance to be on their own for a while."

The evening went all too quickly for all concerned and when the party broke up it seemed very natural for Richard to give Jenny a lift home; when he asked to see her again she was more than happy to say yes.

******

Ben didn't want to get out of bed. His head hurt, his throat hurt, he ached all over, all he wanted to do was go back to sleep for about a week but somebody was pounding on the door and each bang seemed to reverberate inside his head.

Reluctantly he got up and staggered downstairs. As he opened the door a little it was pushed wide and Tony barged past him and went into the sitting room. Ben followed and fell down onto the sofa, putting his head in his hands he let out a groan.

"Did we have a good time last night? I hope we did cos I feel like death today, I hope it was worth it."

Tony grunted. "Huh, you might have thought so last night but today you may change your mind. Just what the hell were you on last night anyway? I've never seen you so spaced out."

16

Ben looked up at him and shrugged. "What's the difference what it was, we had a good time didn't we?"

Tony reached down and grabbed Ben by the scruff of his neck and hauled him up to a mirror hanging over the fireplace. "Take a look in there stupid," he said.

Ben looked in the mirror and saw that he had a huge swelling over the side of his face and a black eye. His top lip was twice as big as normal and there was blood in his hair.

"What happened?" he asked looking at himself in astonishment. "What will I say to Jenny about this?"

"Never mind your sister," replied Tony. "I'm sure you'll think of something to keep her sweet, it's not her you have to worry about, its Sonny Letts and his brother."

Ben swung round to face Tony. "Why should I have to worry about them?"

Tony sat back down on the sofa and lit a cigarette. He leaned back and took a long drag and blowing the smoke towards the ceiling, settled comfortably.

"Last night you were so out of it you wouldn't have know if you were on the moon. That would have been fine but you had to go and make a play for Poppy. You know who I mean don't you? Poppy, the one who goes out with Frank Letts. All night you were all over her and you can guess that she didn't exactly turn you down. Anyway, Frank was getting a bit pissed off with the pair of you and he was going to sort you out but as a favour to me he let you off with a little slapping, otherwise you may not have been able to walk for a while from what he was going to do to you."

Ben went very pale. He realised how near he had come to being really badly beaten. The Letts brothers, Sonny and Frank, ran a nightclub. They were the sort of men you didn't get on the wrong side of. Frank had recently come out of prison and he ran the club with his younger brother.

It wasn't the sort of club to go to if you were looking for a quiet drink. It was the sort of place that catered for most tastes. The police had raided it a few times but never yet had any drugs been found on the premises. The police, however, had their suspicions and were biding their time. The Letts brothers knew how closely they were being watched so at the moment were on their best behaviour. Lucky for Ben.

"I guess I owe you one Tony," said Ben looking a bit shamefaced.

"I'll bear it in mind kid," said Tony. "Now get yourself cleaned up and we can have a hair of the dog."

Ben went into the bathroom to make himself look more presentable. He stared at himself in the mirror.

What a fool he was to try to get off with Poppy of all people, she wasn't even his type. OK maybe she was pretty in a way, that's if you could see her under all that dyed hair. Then there was the make-up and the way she wore her clothes, well it was a wonder she could walk in those skirts and high heels. Still, thinking about it there was something about her. He gave a sigh, thinking to himself he had better put all thoughts of Poppy out of his head if he wanted to stay healthy, after all, as Tony always says, there were plenty more fish in the sea.

He turned on the taps and plunged his head under the cold water.

******

Amanda Armstrong looked at herself in the mirror and decided she looked stunning. She was wearing a long evening dress in deep red velvet; it was low cut with a tight waist. She wore a ruby necklace with a matching bracelet, she was aware how the richness of her dress showed her creamy skin off to its best advantage. On her feet were delicate ruby shoes, a perfect match with her dress.

She adjusted the tiny curls over her forehead and lifted her chin to study her make-up. She wanted to look perfect tonight.

Amanda was used to the best and she usually got it.

Amanda was twenty-four, she was rich, she was beautiful, she was thoroughly spoilt. She knew she was beautiful, it would have been unthinkable to be anything but beautiful because she was the golden girl. All of her life she had been pampered and she accepted it as her right, ageing parents who had long since given up any idea of offspring had hailed her conception as a miracle. Her birth had been the pinnacle of their existence. If her father had secretly wished for a boy, nobody would have guessed.

Amanda was at last satisfied with her appearance, she was the epitome of elegance. Tall, slim, with dark hair piled up onto the top of her head, showing off the graceful curve of her neck. The curls framed her oval face and her eyelashes were thick and long. The only thing that marred her beauty was her mouth, her lips were thin and mostly turned down at the corners, and this would have been an indication as to Amanda's true self had anyone bothered to study her closely.

She picked up the photograph from her dressing table. It was a picture of her and a young man.

They were sitting on sun lounges by the side of a swimming pool, each had a drink in their hand and they were laughing into each other's eyes. The man was tall with dark hair. He had blue eyes and a square chin. His nose was a little on the large size but it didn't look out of place. His mouth was the perfect shape and his teeth were white and even. Amanda had been in love with him for as long as she could remember. His name was Tim Knight. They had known each other all their lives. Both mothers hoped that their children would marry. Both families lived on large estates in the country within reasonably short distance of each other. Tim's father owned a chain of department stores and Tim was getting ready to take up the reins from his father who was hoping to retire in the not too distant future. Although Tim also was an only child he was unlike Amanda insofar as he had charm. He was easy going and happy and totally unaware of the effect he had on women. The fact that he was heir to millions didn't bother him unduly. In fact he preferred to live in his own modest flat in town most of the time. When he was visiting his parents as he was at the moment, it was usual for him to spend time with Amanda and her family.

Amanda put down the photo and left the room, she knew she was just late enough to make an entrance into dinner.

Chapter Two

Jenny was humming to herself as she put the finished touches to the table. Richard should be here any minute now. He was always on time, which was one of the many things Jenny liked about him. As she stood back to admire her efforts the doorbell rang. She ran to open it and there he was with a bunch of flowers in one hand and a bottle of wine in the other.

The cold air made Jenny shiver and she quickly pulled him in.

Putting the flowers into her arms, he gave her a kiss on the cheek and shrugged his coat off. He sniffed the air and opened his eyes wide. "Wow something smells great." Jenny turned and walked into the kitchen, Richard followed.

"Do you realise we have been going out for a year now?" Richard informed her. "Perhaps it's time you made an honest man of me."

Jenny put her arms around his waist and laid her head on his chest. "I like the way things are right now, we don't have to rush into anything do we? Come on lets go and eat or our dinner will be spoilt."

Richard looked down at her and his heart melted. He had loved Jenny from the moment he saw her. He thought she felt the same way at times, but it was as if she was afraid to commit herself. Well he would just have to keep trying; he had no intention of losing her.

They sat at the table and Richard poured the wine. He raised his glass and looked at Jenny. She looked so lovely, she had on a simple black dress and her hair was tied back with a bow. Richard could never get over the effect she had on him. He wanted to be with her all the time. All he could think of was the two of them together. More than anything in the world he wanted her to marry him.

She lifted her glass and clinked it with his, as they were about to drink there was a loud pounding at the door.

Jenny frowned and went to answer it but before she could reach it the pounding started again. She opened the door and her brother fell inside. Jenny jumped back in alarm at the sight of him, then she was down on her knees beside him. He was covered in blood. The doctor's instinct in Richard took over; he lifted Ben in his arms and took him into the lounge. Laying him down on the sofa he called to Jenny to get hot water and towels. By the time she returned with them Richard had Ben's coat and shirt off. He spent the next ten minutes cleaning up the blood.

Jenny sat on a chair watching Richard, she felt sick and helpless.

Richard turned to Jenny and brushing his hair out of his eyes with the back of his hand said, "This wound is too deep, it needs stitching, we must take him to hospital."

At the word hospital Ben's eyes flew open, he looked up at Richard and grabbed his arm. "No," he shouted. "I don't want to go to hospital. I won't go to hospital."

Jenny rose from her chair and knelt beside Ben. She smoothed his hair from his forehead and tried to calm him but he became more and more distraught.

Richard looked at the young man and then seeing the effect it was having on Jenny, left the room, he returned almost immediately pulling on his coat. "I think it will be a good idea if I go home and get my bag. I can easily patch him up. He seemed set against going to hospital." Hearing this, Ben became less agitated. Richard started for the door, calling over his shoulder to Jenny that he would be back soon.

Jenny managed to get Ben upstairs to his bedroom. By the time Richard arrived back with his medical bag Ben was in bed. Richard lost no time in getting to work. Jenny watched him work swiftly and efficiently. It was the first time she had seen him work and she was mesmerised by his hands swiftly pulling together the torn flesh. It needed quite a few stitches. The wound was at the top of Ben's right arm. There were other minor cuts to deal with but Richard made short work of that. Finally it was over and Ben lay back under the covers. He looked up at Richard and Jenny and reaching out for Jenny's hand said, "I'm sorry sis," turning to Richard he said, "thanks Richard, I won't forget this. Sorry I spoilt your dinner too."

Richard rolled down his shirt sleeves and turning to Jenny, took her by the shoulders and gently pushing her to the door said, "What the doctor orders now is some sleep for his patient," and with this he quietly closed the door. Ben turned on his side and closed his eyes. He breathed a big sigh and tried not to think of the past few hours.

Jenny sat on the sofa with Richard, drinking a small whisky. Tonight should have been so special but now everything was ruined. Once again her brother was in trouble, she had no idea what it was all about but it looked serious this time. Richard spoke, almost voicing her thoughts.

"That cut was pretty deep. I thought at first that it was a knife wound but it's not. Do you know where he was tonight?"

Jenny looked at him, she looked pale and tired. "The truth is I never know where he is or what he gets up to. He still hangs out with Tony, I'm so scared that one day he'll get into real trouble."

With this she turned to Richard and burying her face in his chest, burst into tears. Richard put his arms around her and murmured into her hair, "Don't cry my darling, things will look better in the morning. I think the best thing you can do is to get a good nights rest. I'll be round as soon as I can."

Kissing her once again, Richard put on his coat and left. Jenny sat alone feeling miserable. She was tired of being responsible for Ben. Surely it was time he grew up. Slowly she stood up and looking at the untouched meal still on the table, decided it could stay as it was until tomorrow. Quietly she made her way upstairs.

*****

It was eight weeks later and a new year had started. Jenny had the feeling that this year was going to be a good one. It was raining and Jenny shivered as she hurried home. She was looking forward to a long soak in the bath and an early night with a book. Richard was on nights at the hospital so she wouldn't see him for a few days. Yes, things did look as if this was the year for them all. Ben had a job. She didn't know what it was because each time that she asked him about it he evaded giving her an answer. It worried her a little but then everything about Ben worried her so she had made a resolution not to worry over Ben so much in future.

Christmas had been the best one they had celebrated for years. Ben had given her a pearl necklace. If Jenny hadn't known Ben was broke, she would have sworn they were real. He had even bought Richard cuff links. This had pleased Jenny as much as it pleased Richard. The only thing that had spoiled everything was the presence of Tony and Liz. Jenny knew she would never like either of them but she would put up with them for Ben's sake.

As she put her key in the door she could hear music playing. She was surprised because she thought Ben was at work tonight. She hung up her coat and put her umbrella away. It was good to be home. She went to the kitchen and was just about to put the kettle on when a man walked in. At first she thought it was Ben, but when she turned around it was Tony.

Jenny was surprised and a little annoyed to see him there. He came up to her and as usual stood far too close.

"Sorry if I made you jump," he said, looking anything but sorry. "Ben said I could let myself in and pick up something I left here last week. He said to tell you he won't be in tonight."

As he was talking he was edging closer and closer to Jenny who found herself backed up to the edge of the sink. He picked up a strand of hair and twisted it in his fingers.

"You have beautiful hair but it's all wet," he leered. "Why don't you go and change into something dry?"

Jenny pushed his hand away and moved from the sink. She was furious with Ben for giving Tony a key; she would have one or two things to say to him when she saw him.

"If you have what you came for you had better go," she said.

Tony took a step nearer again and picked up her hand. "You don't like me very much do you?" he said. "That's a shame because I've always liked you. We could have some fun together tonight, we have the place to ourselves."

Jenny snatched her hand away. Now she was beginning to feel scared but she would be damned if she would let this little creep know it. Standing as tall as she could she put her hands on her hips and looking him straight in the eyes said in a cool voice, "I think you had better leave." He stood for a moment looking at her; he lifted his hand and ran his fingers down the side of Jenny's face. Jenny stood still, glaring at him. After what seemed hours to Jenny, he turned away and went out. Jenny listened for the door and when she heard it slam behind him she pulled out a chair from under the table and collapsed onto it. She had really been frightened and she was shaking all over.

After a while she got up and made a cup of coffee. At last she began to feel better. She was beginning to feel cold again so she decided to have that long soak in the bath she had promised herself. The music was playing, as it was when she had come home, she decided to leave it on.

The bath felt wonderful. Jenny lay back in the water and let the bubbles soothe her. She began to relax totally. She closed her eyes and sank into the water so that only her head was visible. From downstairs the music was just audible. Jenny felt herself drifting off into that place just before sleep, where everything is soft and tranquil. She thought to herself that this is what it must be like in the womb. She stretched her arms above her head and gave a deep contented sigh. The next second her eyes flew open and she let out a scream. She tried to grab a towel but she was too late.

Tony stood next to the bath with the towel in his hand. He stared down at Jenny and threw the towel away. If Jenny had been frightened earlier, it was as nothing to the sheer terror she felt now.

Tony sat on the edge of the bath and slowly folded his arms.

For a moment, time seemed to stand still for Jenny. It was as if she was looking at some horrible scene in a play.

Then blind fury took over. Crossing her arms over her breasts she shouted at the top of her voice. "What the hell do you think you're doing? Get out at once."

Tony took not the slightest notice of her shouting. Slowly he stood up and very deliberately pulled the plug out of the bath. Jenny watched in silence as the bubbles whirled around as if in a race to empty out. Before the bath was half empty, Jenny was up and out of the bathroom. She had never moved so quickly in her life. Fear had given her wings, but as fast as she was, Tony was faster. Jenny had tried to get to her bedroom but he was there as quick as a flash.

Grabbing her by the wrists he threw her onto the bed. Jenny tried to hide her nakedness with the covers and stared wide-eyed at Tony standing over her. Her brain was working at lightning speed and her heart was beating so fast she could hear it in her head. She was trying so hard to get control of the situation. With a monumental effort she said in a calm voice, "This has gone far enough Tony. Leave now and no one will ever know about this."

Tony sat on the side of the bed. "And I promise you sweetheart that no one will ever know about this, it will be our little secret. Now be nice and we will both have a good time."

Jenny thought that she would be sick if he laid one hand on her. She tried desperately to stay calm and talk to him.

"Please Tony let me get up. Richard will be here soon."

Tony looked at her and from the look on his face she knew she was wasting her time appealing to his better nature.

"Nice try darling but I happen to know he doesn't see you when he works nights. I have been planning this for quite a while but I reckon you were worth the wait." He stood up and slowly started to undress. Jenny sat up and clutching the covers to her tried to reason with him. She was now almost in a state of shock but she knew she must not let him see just how terrified she was.

"Please Tony, please let me go."

As if she wasn't there he carried on undressing. Gathering all her strength Jenny sprang up and tried to get to the door. He moved as quickly as a cat after its prey and was there before her. Now his face changed as he turned the key in the lock. He seemed to tower above her and Jenny felt her legs give way. She thought she was going to faint, if only this nightmare would end. He picked her up as if she were a small child. His strength was a surprise to her; it belied his slim frame. There was no smile on his face now. He threw her on the bed and she felt his weight as he fell onto her.

His face was right in front of her and she could feel his breath on her. Her eyes were inches from his and she could see from his expression that she could expect no mercy.

He lifted her wrists over her head and pinned her arms down. His knees were over her thighs and she was powerless.

As if in slow motion he lowered his head and put his lips to hers. Jenny at once sank her teeth into his lip. He jerked his head up and let out an oath. In a split second he let go of her wrist and slapped her. Quick as a flash he held her captive again. Jenny tasted blood in her mouth. She didn't know if it was hers or his.

"Now if you want to play rough that's alright with me darling, I quite enjoy it that way." She stared up at him. Never had she felt so powerless. She thought of Richard and the tears flooded her eyes. She had wanted him to be the first. She had dreamed of how it would be, romantic and loving. Not like this, oh dear God not like this. She tried to throw his weight off but he seemed half crazed and the more she struggled the more he seemed to enjoy it. He straddled her body and looked down at her.

"I've dreamed of this," he leered, "and the best thing of all is that no one will ever know. Would you like me to tell you why my little darling?"

Jenny was by now incapable of speech. Part of her brain was telling her that this wasn't happening, the other half was desperately trying to think of a way out of this nightmare.

Tony put his mouth next to her ear and whispered to her, "Let me remind you of Christmas sweetheart. Remember that fancy necklace that your baby brother gave you? You said the pearls were so lovely they looked real. You were so pleased with them. Well guess what, they are real. Also your precious Richard's cufflinks are solid gold. Remember that ram-raid on the jeweller's shop just before Christmas? Guess who pulled that off, more to the point, guess who was the driver? It was none other than your little baby brother. Now you understand why you won't tell anyone about this. If you do, your boyfriend will be done for receiving and Ben will end up inside as sure as you're born. Now that's enough talking. Now it's time to be nice to me."

Jenny sat in the corner of her bedroom. She had no idea how long she had been sitting there. She realised she was cold and so she slowly stood up and covered herself with her duvet.

Earlier she had listened to his footsteps running downstairs. He had been whistling as he left. She had locked herself in the bathroom and had bathed over and over again. Never had she felt so humiliated and dirty. After a while she had come out of the bathroom and locked herself in her bedroom. She had lost all track of time. She vaguely thought that Ben might be home at any time, she didn't know how she would ever be able to look him in the face again. How would she ever be able to see Richard again? At the thought of Richard, it was as if a dam had burst. Her tears flowed down her cheeks and she cried as if her heart would break. She cried for all the dreams she had that now could never come true. She cried for the way Ben had betrayed her. She cried for her violated body. She must have fallen asleep at some time. The next thing she knew, it was dark; Jenny stood up and again went to the bathroom. An hour later, Jenny dressed herself and went downstairs. She made herself a cup of tea and as she sipped the hot liquid she started to feel warmth flowing back into her body.

The telephone rang, making Jenny jump and spill the hot tea in her lap. She took no notice and eventually the phone stopped ringing. She poured herself another cup of tea and began to feel a little better. Her next feelings were anger. She was angry with Ben, he had always been spoilt and because she had tried to take the place of their mother, he had repaid her by ruining her life. She was angry with Tony and she could see no way that she would be able to go to the police if he had been telling the truth about the robbery at the jewellers shop, but most of all, she was angry with herself. Why couldn't she just go to the police and to hell with Ben? She was tired of looking after him. Since the death of their parents she had tried to protect Ben. It was time to let him stand on his own two feet. She deserved to have a life without worrying over her brother all the time. Then she remembered what Tony had said about the cuff links that Ben had given Richard for Christmas. If they were stolen, how would that effect him? Would his career be ruined because of it? Jenny's brain was spinning. She wished desperately that her mother was here. If only there was somebody she could turn to. She didn't know what to do. Jenny's body ached all over and her head was pounding. Jenny had no idea what to do next. A hundred different thoughts whirled round and round her head. She felt as if she was in some terrible nightmare and she was unable to wake up.

The telephone rang again and Jenny still could not answer it. She realised that it was Richard and at the thought of him, she once again wept. Finally she realised that she was exhausted, she stood up and walked over to the kitchen dresser and took a dustbin liner out of a draw, then she made her way up the stairs. When she entered her bedroom, she tore the bed linen off and bundled it into the bag. She knew it would be no good washing the bed linen, it had to be destroyed. Never again would she be able to use it, as far as she was concerned it was contaminated. When she had made up the bed, she collapsed down onto it. Mercifully, because of sheer exhaustion, she fell into a deep sleep.

The next day, Jenny woke up and thought for a minute it had all been a dreadful nightmare until she sat up and her body told her that it had been no dream but a hideous reality.

There beside the bed were the soiled bedclothes. She stared at them for a while and then she sprang out of bed and grabbing hold of the bag ran down the stairs and out of the kitchen, and pulling off the dustbin lid she thrust the bag into the bin. She then went back indoors and upstairs to the bathroom and once again started to run a bath. As she lay back in the bubbles she decided that she would be strong and try as much as she could to get over what had happened without telling anyone. She prayed that she would be able to get through this. She knew it wouldn't be easy but it was the only thing she could do if she wanted to stop herself from going completely mad. She would need all her strength to get through the days ahead and all the days after.

Chapter Three

Amanda Armstrong watched the bubbles in her champagne chasing each other to the top of the glass. She was sitting in front of a roaring fire and by her side was Tim Knight. Although she had been with Tim all day she was feeling petulant. It was her birthday and she had been hinting for months that she would like an engagement ring, it seemed to go completely over Tim's head.

Tim sensed she was in a mood. He was now aware of the way Amanda felt about him, but the truth was he didn't feel the same way. He leaned over and gave her a gentle push on the shoulder.

"Hey birthday girl, why the long face? You know you'll get wrinkles?"

Amanda pouted and looked sideways at him. "I was thinking of Mummy. She was half expecting us to make an announcement at dinner tonight. I'm sure your parents were too."

Tim sighed and stood up. He didn't want a confrontation tonight but on the other hand he thought it was time to settle this once and for all. He was tired of the innuendoes from the two families. As far as he was concerned there could never be any romance between them. Gently he took the glass from Amanda's hand and put it on the coffee table. He took her hands and pulled her up. She held her breath and waited for what he was about to say, it was not what she wanted to hear.

"Amanda, we have know each other all of our lives. You know that I love you as if you were my sister. You will always be my best friend and I know you think of me as a big brother. I'll always be here for you."

He was quite aware she didn't think of him as a brother but it was the best way that he could think of to clear the air without hurting her feelings.

Amanda pulled away from him and gave a nervous laugh. She was devastated at hearing Tim say what she had always dreaded to hear. She was suddenly furious with him. How dare he, she could have her pick of a score of young men. The trouble was she didn't want anyone but Tim. For the first time in her life she couldn't have what she wanted. No, he couldn't mean it. She would get him if it took a lifetime, he would change his mind. His words had stabbed her heart but she would never show how much she was hurting.

"Well then big brother I think we had better call it a day. It's been fun but it's rather late and a girl needs her beauty sleep you know."

Reaching up, she gave him a peck on the cheek and feigning a long yawn, left the room.

When she reached her bedroom she threw herself down on her bed and punched the pillows in anger. She would have liked to cry but she was far too angry. She sat up and lifted her arm to examine the bracelet adorning her wrist. Tim had given it to her for her birthday. When she had seen the small box her heart had stood still. She had thought that at last Tim had bought her an engagement ring. When she had seen the bracelet she had wanted to throw it back in his face. Instead she had thanked him and kissed him lightly on the cheek. Now she tore it off and threw it away from her.

By the time Amanda went down for breakfast the next morning, Tim had already left along with his parents. There was only her mother seated at the dining table finishing her third cup of coffee. Amanda sat down and poured herself a cup. Her mother glanced at her and knew by the expression on Amanda's face that she was not in a sociable mood. It wasn't hard to guess the reason for the sulky look on her daughter's face.

Mrs Elizabeth Armstrong waited for her daughter to speak but Amanda stared into her coffee and remained silent. Mrs Armstrong cleared her throat and Amanda looked up. "Tim asked me to tell you he was sorry he missed you this morning but he would be delighted if you and I would call in to see him today. We could all have coffee together. I told him we may visit the store." Amanda nodded and put down her cup.

"Fine, if that's what you want, but I don't want to spend all day shopping. I want to go for a ride later. I haven't been for a while and I think Star will be getting a bit lazy."

Star was the name of her newest horse. Amanda had a passion for riding. She had first owned her own pony at the age of four. All her life she had been around horses and she was an expert in the saddle.

Mrs Armstrong pushed back her chair and stood up. "I'll have the car made ready in fifteen minutes then. Don't keep me waiting."

Mrs Armstrong sat in front of her dressing table and frowned at her reflection. She had been very disappointed this morning. She had been expecting Amanda to have an engagement ring on her finger by now. Last night everything had gone well and she and her husband, along with Tim's parents, had retired early so that the young couple could be alone.

Amanda's father had left instructions to be told immediately if there was good news this morning.

What was the matter with them? What was it they were waiting for? She had been married by the time she was Amanda's age. She would have to try to get to the bottom of this sooner or later, but for now she had better ring the chauffeur and order the car. Getting up, she walked over to the telephone.

Arriving at the store, Amanda and her mother went straight up to Tim's office. He was standing at the window when his secretary showed them in. He came over to them and gave each one a kiss on the cheek.

"Come and sit down Aunt Elizabeth," he said. "I was just thinking about last night, I'm afraid I over indulged again. I will either have to give up your wonderful dinners or spend more time down the gym."

Mrs Armstrong merely looked sideways at him and sat on the proffered chair.

Amanda, however, walked over to the window and looked down at the street below. "I will never understand how you can bear to work in the city Tim," she said. "I always find it so depressing."

"That my dearest is because you are spoilt rotten and spend all your time either on a horse or looking for other diversions, which I might add is not difficult for you. Some of us like to work. Anytime you fancy joining the working classes, I could offer you a job."

Amanda turned from the window and walked over to Tim. She brushed an imaginary speck off his lapel and looked up into his face. She pouted in what she thought was a sexy way and putting both arms around his neck said, "No disrespects darling but can you ever imagine me working here as some little shop girl?"

He laughed down into her face; there was no way on earth that Amanda would ever consider working for a living. Especially in father's store. He reached up and gently took her arms from his neck.

"No disrespects to you darling but can you ever imagine me employing you?"

They both laughed at the idea of it. Mrs Armstrong sat watching them both. Once again she was filled with a feeling of bewilderment. Here were two delightful young people that clearly got on well together. What on earth was stopping them from getting together? They made such a handsome couple. She was sure Amanda wanted Tim so it must be Tim that was holding back. She knew her husband was beginning to lose patience with Tim. That was because he doted on Amanda and he felt that his beloved daughter was being taken for granted. Elizabeth Armstrong knew her daughter better than her father; Amanda was not the type to be taken for granted. Elizabeth was suddenly aware that she was being spoken to. Tim was smiling down at her, she thought again what a perfect son-in-law he would be.

"I asked if you would like some coffee Aunt Elizabeth? You seem miles away."

"Coffee would be lovely thank you darling. In fact I was wondering when you were going to offer. I hope you have some of those delicious biscuits to go with it."

He bent down and quickly kissed the top of her head. "Now would I let my favourite lady go shopping in my store without sustenance? You shall have coffee immediately and as many biscuits as you wish Madame." So saying, he picked up the telephone to order.

Amanda sat on the corner of his desk and took out a cigarette. She knew Tim didn't like her smoking but she was still angry with him. Tim however, ignored this action. He wasn't going to be drawn into an argument about smoking today. Instead he walked over to a cupboard and found her an ashtray. She was aware that she had lost yet another minor battle and so she inhaled just once and angrily stubbed out the cigarette. She suddenly wished she had stayed at home today. She would have been much happier spending today with Star. When she was in the saddle, she could forget everything and give herself up to the sheer joy of being in control of an animal with such strength and speed as her wonderful horse. At least Star would never let her down.

She looked at Tim and all at once her anger left her and she was filled with unhappiness. She loved him with all her heart. What was the reason for his reluctance to commit himself? Never did it occur to

Amanda that he just didn't love her. How could he not love her, she was beautiful, rich and intelligent, she had everything. Maybe he wanted to get established in the store a bit more before he proposed. Yes, that was it, he would ask her to marry him very soon she was sure.

There was a knock on the door and Tim's secretary entered with a tray. Tim made room for it on his desk and she put it down. She politely said good morning to the ladies and left. Tim picked up the percolator and looking at Amanda said with a smile, "Shall I be mother?"

Amanda found herself unable to resist his smile. Her heart gave a little jig and she found she was smiling back at him, her eyes were soft and she said in the same tone of voice he had used, "This I must see." And without taking her eyes off him she sat down in his chair.

Mrs Armstrong watched him pour the coffee; she took a biscuit and said in a loud voice, "I don't care who will be mother, just as long as it's soon." She didn't see the look of annoyance her daughter gave her.

Chapter Four

Amanda and her mother stepped out of the lift into the fashion department. They automatically made for the designer gowns. Amanda didn't really want to buy any new clothes, for once she was in no mood for shopping. The remark Tim had made about her being spoilt still rankled. Her mother was blissfully unaware that her daughter was still sulking, she was already lost among a sea of silks and velvet. A bright splash of colour caught her eye and she pulled it out. She turned to Amanda and held it out to her.

"Try this on darling, I think the colour would suit you."

Amanda took the gown from her and went into a cubicle. Ten minutes later she walked out and stood in front of her mother.

Elizabeth Armstrong gasped at the vision in front of her. The dress had looked quite ordinary before but once on it was a transformation. The colour was such a deep pink it was almost red. It was not the usual plunging neckline that Amanda mostly wore, the gown couldn't have been simpler. It was high at the neck, the waist fitted tightly and then fell away perfectly into soft folds to the floor. Amanda looked at herself in the mirror and was surprised and delighted at what she saw. Her mother was right it did suit her. It made her look fragile and very elegant. She lifted up her hair and turned round admiring the curve of her neck and the way the colour made her skin take on a glow. It made her eyes look even darker and sultry. She laughed at her reflection.

She looked stunning. As she was admiring her reflection she noticed an assistant standing behind her. Amanda was at once struck by the colour of the young woman's hair. She would love to have hair like that. Imagine this gown with that colour hair. She turned round and stared the assistant in the face. She thought how pale the girl looked; she had deep smudges under her eyes as if she hadn't slept.

The assistant smiled at Amanda and said, "That looks as if it were made for you Madam."

Amanda totally ignored her and turning to her mother said, "I think I'll take this, I will need to find shoes and a bag to match. Just let me get out of this."

Jenny waited outside the cubicle for the customer. She felt very ill and worried. She had made a monumental effort to act normally this morning. She was well aware of the looks she had been getting from her colleagues all morning. Mrs Jenkins had asked if she wanted to go home because she looked unwell but the last thing Jenny wanted was to go home. Tina had wanted to know what was wrong but Jenny had said everything was fine and quickly changed the subject.

The curtains were pulled back and the customer threw the gown at Jenny as she swept past.

Jenny shook the gown and asked, "Does Madam wish to buy the gown?"

Amanda gave a nod in answer to the question and Jenny walked over to the counter to wrap up the gown. She picked up some tissue paper to wrap it in and as she was about to fold it she noticed there was a mark on the front. She knew immediately that it was lipstick. This was all she needed today, especially with a customer as awkward as this one. She held up the gown and said, "Oh dear, there seems to be a mark down the front, it looks like lipstick."

Amanda had no doubt that it was her lipstick but she was damned if she would let this shop assistant tell her about it. She looked closely at the offending mark. Jenny gave a bright smile and said, "Not to worry madam, I'm sure it will come out quite easily."

Amanda glared at Jenny and said, "Are you inferring that I soiled the dress?"

Jenny felt herself going red. She didn't feel able to cope with this today. She looked at the immaculately dressed woman in front of her and her heart sank. "I didn't mean to imply anything of the sort Madam, I was just trying to be helpful."

By now Amanda was bored with the whole idea of shopping and she had lost all interest in the gown anyway but she wanted to teach this little shop girl a lesson. She took a diary out of her handbag and without a word to Jenny leaned over and read the name on the badge Jenny wore on her lapel. She wrote it down very slowly, enjoying the power of watching the colour flood the girl's face. Her mother cleared her throat in embarrassment but Amanda took no notice. She turned to her mother and said, "I think I will pay Tim another visit. Are you coming Mother?" With that she turned and headed for the lifts. Her mother looked at Jenny and gave her a little smile, shrugged her shoulders and followed in the wake of her daughter.

*****

Tim stood at the window in his office staring down at the street below. He was not seeing the traffic or the people going about their everyday business, he was seeing a pair of green eyes set in a pale face, surrounded by the most glorious colour hair. The store had been closed for over an hour but Tim was unaware of the time.

That afternoon he had been interrupted by Amanda who had stormed in and demanded that he dismiss one of his staff. He had tried to calm her down and finally had the whole story, at least Amanda's side of it. Later he had sent for the assistant that had been the reason for Amanda's outburst. He had been sitting behind his desk and when the door had opened and he looked on the face of the young woman standing there, his heart had jumped so violently he was sure she must have noticed.

He had to concentrate very hard on what she was saying. He didn't want to talk; he had the wildest urge to hold her in his arms and take away that frightened look on her face. He wanted to sit her down near him and ask all about her life. He wanted to take her hand and hold it and look into those glorious eyes. Never in his whole life had he felt what he was feeling now. he had finally got the whole story of the soiled gown from Jenny. He was inclined to believe her side of the story because he knew Amanda and her prima donna ways only too well. There was no way that he was going to dismiss this girl. Even if she had been rude to Amanda he would have found an excuse not to fire her. As it was, he was sure the fault lay with his spoilt girlfriend and so he had assured the young lady who had been looking at him with eyes that were moist with unshed tears, that she would hear no more of the matter. Mrs Jenkins had earlier given her a glowing report and had assured Tim that Miss Woods was an asset to the store.

Reluctantly Tim had told Miss Woods that she should return to her department and since then he had done not a scrap of work.

The telephone rang bringing him back to the present. It was Amanda. He was in no mood to listen to her at the moment, she would want all the details of this afternoon's talk with Miss Woods. He didn't want to discuss it with her, he made the excuse that he was late for a meeting with his father and rang off as soon as he could. He would tell her mother the outcome of it but not now.

He had forgotten about Amanda before he had put down the phone. Once again he was seeing that face. He realised that he was in love. It made no sense at all. He wasn't the type of man that fell in love at one glance. He had never believed in it before. Things like that just didn't happen, especially to men like him. What was he to do now? He was the steady, quiet type, not the type that fell for a pair of green eyes and a figure like a goddess. This was so unlike everything he believed in. How could he feel like this after meeting her just once? Jenny, Jenny, he kept saying her name over and over again to himself. He was acting like an adolescent schoolboy. If this was how it felt to be in love then he was not so sure he liked it. He suddenly realised that it was getting late. He went to get his coat and made his way down to his car.

It was cold, dark and raining as he turned his car out of the car park. He drove down the busy street and stopped at a red light. He glanced sideways as he was waiting for the lights to change and as he did so found himself looking at the face that had haunted him all afternoon. She was standing at a bus stop and she looked wet and cold. Without thinking he opened the passenger door and called to her.

Jenny was shivering at the bus stop when the big black jaguar had stopped at the lights. She was amazed when the door opened and her name was called, "Miss Woods, may I offer you a lift? You look soaked through." Jenny recognised Mr Tim Knight. She had only seen him once or twice from a distance since she had worked at the store and now in the same day she had spoken with him twice.

She didn't have much time to answer as the lights were turning green and he was urging her to "hop in quickly."

Jenny got into the car. It was so warm inside. She had been waiting for ages for a bus and she was tired, wet and cold. It had been a horrible day. Now she sat upright and stared ahead. She had no idea what to say to this man. She felt embarrassed and shy.

Tim on the other hand couldn't believe his luck. To find her waiting for a bus seemed the ideal way of an excuse to stop. He glanced sideways at her and again his heart did a somersault. He cleared his throat and said, "Have you been waiting long for a bus?" then felt stupid for voicing such an obvious fact.

Jenny looked at him and nodded. "Yes I missed my usual one, it must have been early."

He smiled. "No wonder you look so cold." He was aware of her sitting so tense and upright. He wanted to put her at ease but he couldn't find words to say. Then he realised that he didn't know where he was going. He looked at her and asked where she lived.

Jenny gave him the name of her road; she was surprised when he told her he knew it. It would take about twenty minutes to get there and Jenny was by now ridged with embarrassment.

Tim on the other hand was trying to get his brain to work. He didn't want to drop her at her house and just go home. He would like to just drive all night with her sitting beside him.

There was silence in the car for about ten minutes, if he didn't think of something soon she would be home and it would be too late. Taking the bull by the horns he said, "I don't suppose you would like to have a drink with me would you? It's been a hell of a day for me and I would like to unwind a bit. I know a very nice little pub just off the next street. I don't usually go around asking young ladies out like this either but it would be nice if you did." He thought, my god man you're jabbering like an idiot.

Jenny wouldn't usually accept an invitation from a man that she didn't know but there was something about this one. She believed him when he said he didn't ask women out very much.

On impulse she turned and said, "I suppose I could do with a drink. I have also had a hell of a day."

A big smile lit up Tim's face at her answer. A few minutes later he was pulling into the car park of the pub.

The bar was warm and welcoming. It was quiet at this time of the evening. At the far end of the room there was a huge open fireplace with a roaring fire blazing. There were copper pots and kettles that reflected the glow from the fire, which gave off a delightful smell from the burning logs. They seated themselves at a table near the fire and Tim went off to get the drinks. When he came back they sat in silence for a while, sipping their drinks and feeling the glow from the fire slowly warming and relaxing them. Neither of them spoke for some time but each was aware of the other. They were both staring into the fire. It soothed them and gave them both a feeling of peace.

As if a signal had been given they both started to talk at once, then both stopped.

Jenny laughed for the first time in days. Tim was captivated all over again.

"You go first," he said.

Jenny smiled. "I was only going to say I'm glad you gave me a lift. I would also like you to know I don't usually get in the car of strangers either."

He smiled back. "I'm glad I gave you a lift too. Look, I know they serve very good food here and I feel hungry all of a sudden. Why don't we both have dinner here?"

Jenny realised that she was hungry also. It seemed quite natural to accept. She hadn't wanted to go home; in fact she thought she would never feel safe there again. Now here she was, sitting with her boss of all people and feeling as if they were old friends. He seemed to have the power to make her relax and feel safe.

She looked into his eyes and with a start realised that she didn't feel safe at all. She felt aware of something going on that she was helpless to stop. Something that was quite out of the ordinary. Not even with Richard had she ever experienced the feelings she now had each time this man looked into her eyes. She felt herself going red and she became flustered.

Tim reached out and put his hand over hers as it lay on the table. To both of them it was like a bolt of lightning. She looked into his eyes and saw into his soul. He leaned over to her and when his lips tenderly brushed hers it was as if she had waited all her life for this moment. He sat back and looked at her.

"You know what's happened don't you?"

She looked at him and slowly nodded.

For a while they sat in silence, holding hands and trying to make sense of it. Jenny couldn't believe it. Things like this just didn't happen. How could she feel like this? She had just suffered the worst experience of her life. It should have put her off men for good. Then there was Richard. He wanted to marry her. They had been going out together for ages, but as she looked at the face of the man across the table, she knew that Richard could be nothing more than a friend from now on.

Tim let out a deep breath. "I don't know what you have done to me my darling but it's rocked my world. I feel as if I'm on a different planet."

Again they fell silent. Both were aware that there would be problems ahead.

*****

The next day, Tim sent a note down to Jenny, asking if she would come up to his office after work. Jenny didn't have too much difficulty over this with her colleagues. They all thought it was about the incident with the gown. Tina had wanted to wait for her but Jenny had persuaded her not to. As soon as the store had closed, Jenny waited until Tina had left, then she put on her coat and made her way up to Tim's office. She knocked on the door and he opened it immediately, as if he had been standing behind the door waiting for her.

He pulled her into his arms and kissed her. Jenny's arms went around his neck and she kissed him back, matching his passion. He let go of her and brushed a strand of her hair away from her eyes.

"You can't imagine how much I have waited to do that," he said.

Jenny closed her eyes and gave a sigh. "Oh I think I can," she answered.

He pulled her over to a seat and gently sat her down.

"I still think this is a dream," he told her.

Jenny nodded. "I can't take it all in either. So much has happened to me in the last week, things that I haven't told to anyone. Now I don't know what to do anymore."

Tim looked into her face and saw she looked frightened. He took her hands in his and said, "What's making you look so worried my darling? Don't you know that I will do anything in the world to make you happy? It seems as if I have waited a lifetime for you and now that I've found you I don't intend to let you go."

Jenny found herself thinking of the nightmare she had suffered at the hands of that loathsome Tony. Once again she felt dirty and degraded. What would Tim say if he knew her terrible secret? Would he turn from her in disgust? Then there was Richard. She was supposed to be seeing him tonight but she had put him off. She felt her face redden and she pulled her hands away and stood up.

"Maybe we are moving too fast," she said. "You really don't know anything about me, nor I you."

Tim took her by the shoulders and turned her to him. "I know that I have fallen madly in love with you and that I won't let anyone or anything come between us. I expect people will gossip at first. You will have to go through more than me I suppose. Once everyone hears about us they will have a field day but we can ignore the rest of the world. As long as you love me my darling I will make sure you are happy."

He ran his fingers through his hair and sat on the edge of his desk.

"Maybe I'm being selfish, after all it's you that will be in the firing line. The staff won't dare say anything to me about us whereas you may be in for some backbiting. Is that what's worrying you darling? If it is, I can assure you that won't be allowed to happen. Come on now, I suggest you let me take you to dinner. There are lots of things I have to tell you."

Jenny stood up and tried to smile but the remark he had made about the staff, suddenly brought home to her that they came from different worlds. He was the heir to millions and she was a working girl. How on earth would it ever work?

Chapter Five

The following weeks were some of the most difficult Jenny had ever spent. She was filled with a whirlpool of emotion. She had fallen in love so quickly and so completely that it frightened her. She knew that Tim felt the same and the time they spent together seemed only to forge a deeper bond between them.

She had told him about Richard and he had agreed that she should tell him face to face that she was ending their relationship.

She was on her way to meet him in the park. There was a promise of spring in the air but Jenny didn't notice any of it. For a while now she had been feeling quite ill. That wasn't surprising given all that had happened in her life recently. Today she wanted to be anywhere but on her way to meet Richard. He had been a tower of strength for her whenever Ben had been in trouble.

Jenny looked ahead and there was Richard already waiting for her. He was seated on a bench beside the pond, watching a family of mallards swimming and calling out to each other with the most extraordinary loud noises.

She stood still for a moment and watched him. He was such a good man. Why couldn't she have fallen in love with him? She knew he would be so hurt but she was powerless to help herself from loving Tim.

She started to walk towards him and was about to call his name when everything started to go black. With each step she took she seemed to be walking into the ground.

Richard turned and saw her and quickly ran to her. He was just in time to catch her; she collapsed into his arms in a faint.

He put her onto the bench and she came round almost immediately. She sat up and tried to stand but she was again overcome with dizziness. Her stomach hurt and she wanted to be sick. She felt so ill that she closed her eyes and ignored Richard's frantic questions.

Richard was very worried at the state Jenny was in, she seemed to be in a lot of pain. Her pulse was racing and she looked as if she was going to pass out again. He decided the best thing would be to run her into the hospital himself.

*****

Richard was pacing up and down the hospital corridor waiting for news of Jenny. He felt as if he had been there for days. Now he understood how his patients felt waiting for news of their loved ones.

His name was called out and he turned to see a colleague of his beckoning to him. He pushed aside the curtain and entered the cubicle.

Jenny was looking very scared and helpless. Richard felt so much love for her. He took her hand and put it to his lips.

"How are you feeling now darling? You gave me quite a scare." He brushed the hair from her temple and looked up at the young doctor standing beside Jenny.

The doctor knew Richard and Jenny were an item, in fact they had met socially before. He gave Richard a smile and said very gently, "She is still in some pain but she will be fine. I'm really sorry to tell you Richard that she has lost the baby, I expect you would like to be alone for a while, you know where to find me."

Richard was stunned. He looked at Jenny; she was staring at him.

She looked as shocked as he was. For a while neither of them could speak. Richard couldn't take in what he had just been told.

Jenny couldn't have lost a baby. She was never pregnant. There must be some ghastly mix up. He sat in a chair and put his head in his hands. His mind was telling him that no doctor would make that sort of mistake, while his heart was telling him his beloved Jenny would never betray him in that way. He would have staked his life on it.

This was the woman he wanted to spend his life with. The woman who wanted to wait until they were married before they went to bed together.

A picture came into his mind of his Jenny in the arms of another man and he experienced a pain so strong it made him cry out.

Jenny looked at him. Never had she seen such raw agony as she now saw etched on his face. Nothing she could say would make him feel any better now. She wanted to reach out to him but she had no right to do so now. She wanted to tell him everything, scream out that she had been raped. It wasn't her fault, it wasn't her fault.

Richard didn't know how long he sat there. His mind had gone blank. He felt numb.

Very slowly he stood up and looked down at Jenny. He said one word, "Who?"

Jenny just shook her head and closed her eyes. The tears rolled down her face as she heard Richard leave.

*****

Tony sat on a stool at the bar. He had been eyeing up a blonde at the other end of the bar but she didn't seem interested. Never mind, the night was still young. He looked at his watch and frowned.

Ben should have been here by now. He was beginning to get fed up with Ben lately; he would have to watch him. It looked as if he was going soft. He worried far too much about his big sister.

At the thought of Ben's sister, a smile came to his face.

Now there was a woman. Maybe it was about time that he paid her another visit. He had thought about her constantly since the night that he had visited her. He still saw Liz but she was not in the same league as Jenny. Jenny had class.

He glanced up and saw Ben heading in his direction.

Ben sat on a stool beside Tony. He looked dishevelled and anxious.

Tony ordered more drinks from the barmaid and turned to Ben. "You're late," he snapped. "Didn't you keep a decent watch for yourself from that jeweller's job?"

Ben looked horrified. "Shut up," he hissed, "someone will hear you."

Tony threw back his head and laughed. "Do you think there's anyone in here that would give a shit if they did hear? Anyway it might do your reputation a bit of good."

Ben looked around him and realised for the first time how shabby the place really was. He had once thought that this was an exciting way to spend time but now he was seeing it as it really was. He looked at the people sitting at tables or at the bar and saw them as they really were.

The whole place was shabby. There was a stage at one end of the room. It had grubby red velvet curtains with gold braid trimmings that were falling off in places. The tables were littered with overflowing ashtrays. A few couples were on the dance floor lumbering round to the strains of the latest pop record played by a bored and mediocre disc jockey. Ben pushed back his stool and stood up.

"I'm not in the mood for this tonight Tony. I think it's time I went home."

Tony's jaw dropped in surprise as Ben turned and headed for the exit.

Tony followed him outside. He caught up with Ben and pulled his sleeve making him stop. "What the hell is up with you tonight?"

Ben turned up his coat collar and reached in his pocket for a cigarette. He inhaled deeply. "I guess I'm just worried about my sister. She has just come out of hospital and she looks awful. She said it was just women's problems but she looks so miserable. On top of that she and Richard seem to have split up."

"That's a good move on her part I would say. I never did like that stuck up sod," said Tony. Ben was lost in thought. Jenny had been acting strangely lately. At one time he had been quite frightened by the way she had looked. Then, later she seemed to perk up and was really happy, now this. Still he supposed it was the way women were. Not much point in trying to figure them out. He gave a sigh.

"Oh stuff it," he said, "let's go somewhere decent for a change."

"Now you're talking kiddo," said Tony, "and I know just the place."

Ben grinned at him and suddenly felt a lot happier.

The next day Ben woke up at Tony's place feeling far from happy.

*****

Jenny turned the key in the lock and let herself in. She had been to see her doctor and he had agreed that she was able to go back to work now.

She went into the kitchen and put the kettle on. The telephone rang and she knew it would be Tim. She stood for a moment undecided whether to answer it or not. She hadn't seen him for over two weeks and she ached to hear his voice. The longing became too much for her and she ran to answer it. Just as she got to it, however, it stopped ringing. She sighed and went back into the kitchen. She had almost made up her mind never to see him again but she might just as well try to stop breathing. She had fought battles with herself since she had lost the baby. That had been the biggest shock of her life. Jenny had never thought about becoming pregnant after she had been raped. The first few days had been the worst of her life. She had even thought of committing suicide. After four days of torment she literally blanked it out. Only then could she cope. The first day she had returned to work she had to cope with that awful woman that had soiled the gown. Still, it had led to her meeting Tim.

It was as if he had been sent to her to make up for all of the bad things that had happened to her. She loved him so much but she was in turmoil about what to tell him. She had phoned Tim from the hospital the day after she had been admitted and told him she was feeling ill and was at home with the flu. She had quite a fight on her hands for a while because he had wanted to come and visit. In the end she had persuaded him to stay away because she said she didn't want him to see her looking a wreck. She had told the same story to Tina but she couldn't tell Ben so she had said it was women's problems. That had worked well enough. The phone rang again and this time she lost no time in answering it.

His voice made her feel weak. How could she think of giving up this man?

"Darling," he said, "How are you feeling? I can't go on any longer without seeing you. I don't care what you look like. Even if you've grown warts on the end of your nose I must see you."

Jenny laughed for the first time in days. "I'm all better darling. I can't wait to see you, warts and all."

"Wonderful," he answered. "We can go out for dinner tonight that's if it's OK with you. What time shall I call for you?"

"About eight," Jenny told him, "and if you can't remember the way just follow the smell of roses. I seem to have enough to open a florist."

Tim laughed. "I must be in love, see you later." He blew her a kiss and rang off.

Jenny sat for a while gazing into space. He made her feel so special. The front door opened and Ben walked in. He looked at his sister and thought how much better she was looking. She smiled at him and he noticed her eyes were sparkling once again. It had been ages since she had looked like that.

"You look better sis," he said. She gave him a quick hug.

"I feel better thanks. Are you staying in tonight? If you are you'll have to see to yourself because I'm going out with Tim."

Ben shrugged his shoulders and flopped into a chair. "That's fine by me. I'm going out later anyway, with Tony." Jenny frowned and sat down near to Ben.

"Why do you keep seeing that man? You know what I think of him. I don't want you to go near him again. I mean it Ben. I don't want you to see him ever again; I don't want him within a mile of this house. He's no good. He'll get you into a load of trouble. Stay away from him."

Ben looked at Jenny. Her hands were gripping the arms of the chair and her face once again looked drawn and white. He didn't understand the intensity of her feelings. He knew she didn't like Tony but she had never reacted like this before at the mention of his name.

He stood up and went over to her and sitting on the edge of her chair took her hands in his. "Calm down Jenny. It's not that big a deal. I don't know why you're getting so worked up over it. Go and get ready for your date."

Jenny jumped out of her seat as if she had been stung, she started pacing the floor then swung round and yelled at Ben. "How can I go out and leave you knowing you are going out with that animal."

Ben's mouth flew open in amazement. Jenny was acting in a way that was so unlike her. To call Tony an animal was going a bit far. She was totally out of order.

He stood up and going over to her took hold of her arms so that she was forced to stand still.

"Jenny what is it with you? You know I see Tony all the time. Why did you call him an animal? I know you have never liked him but you've never been like this before. Either tell me what's wrong or back off."

Jenny drew away from him. She wanted to tell him why but she was too scared. Instead she just looked into his face, then she gently put her hands up and cupped his face saying softly, "I'm sorry Ben. I didn't mean to rant on like that. Put it down to stress. Forgive me?"

Ben gave her a hug. "Nothing to forgive sis. Now go and get ready will you," he pushed her gently towards the door. She turned and looked at him.

"I still don't like him Ben and I mean it when I say I don't want him here ever again." She turned and left the room, leaving Ben wondering what on earth had made her so hostile towards Tony.

Upstairs, Jenny sat on the bed trembling. Would she ever feel normal again? She tried all the time to forget about that awful night but she was still having nightmares over it. If only she could tell somebody about it.

At times she would make up her mind to report it. Then she would think of a hundred reasons why she couldn't. She hated the thought of him getting away with it but she must protect Ben. If he had been involved in that robbery then Tony would make sure the police would know about it were she to tell about the rape.

There was also Richard to think of. He knew nothing of any of this but as far as Jenny knew, he still had the cufflinks. Jenny had gotten rid of her necklace. She couldn't bear to touch it now. The police might think Richard was mixed up with Tony. She couldn't take that chance. She still felt deeply sad over Richard. She hadn't seen him since that awful day in the hospital. She could still see the look on his face.

He had done so much for her and Ben. He must have felt so betrayed and hurt that day. Jenny looked at her watch. She had better start to get ready to go out.

She went to her wardrobe and took out a black dress. She held it up against her and saw her pale face looking back at her. She gave a sigh and whispered to herself, "Thank God for make-up."

She threw the dress on the bed and went to have a shower.

Chapter Six

Just under an hour later Jenny was downstairs waiting for Tim to arrive. Looking out of the window she saw his car pull up outside her door. She ran to the door and pulled it open just as Tim was about to knock. His eyes lit up at the sight of her and he pulled her into his arms.

For a minute neither of them spoke, content to be in each other's arms.

Tim stood back and looked into her face. He had been so worried about her. She looked a little pale still but she was as beautiful as ever.

Gently he tilted up her chin and looked into her eyes. He saw the reflection of his own love looking back at him and it took his breath away.

"It's so good to see you again my darling," he said. "It seems so long since I saw you I was beginning to think you were just a figment of my imagination."

Jenny threw back her head and laughed. It was so good to be in his arms again. All the doubts vanished as she looked into his eyes. Now she was certain this man was the only one for her. She knew she could put the past behind her and look to the future with confidence. Here was a man that loved her as she loved him. He made her feel safe. Nothing could hurt her now.

"I missed you so much," she said.

Tim kissed her again and then pushing her gently away said, "Hurry up and put your coat on. I want to take you back to that pub where we had our first date. I have something special on the menu."

Jenny quickly got her coat and bag and they were on their way.

They were seated at the same table as on that first night. The fire was still burning. The logs gave off that wonderful smell and the copper still gleamed in the glow of the fire.

It was is if they had gone back in time to that first magical night they had found each other. Jenny gave a big sigh and stared into the fire. Tim reached over and took her hand.

"What was that big sigh for?"

Jenny smiled. "That my darling was sheer contentment." Tim put her fingers to his lips and kissed them.

"I know just how you feel my angel. Now if you don't mind there is something I need to ask you."

He put his hand in his pocket and pulled out a small box. He placed it on the table in front of Jenny and opened the lid. Jenny gasped, as she looked at the ring resplendent on the blue velvet. It was the most magnificent diamond solitaire. Its brilliance burst out, dazzling Jenny as she stared in wonder. Tim picked up her hand and slipped the ring on her finger. Jenny couldn't take her eyes off the rainbow of colour that was dancing on her hand. It was as if it were on fire. Never had she seen anything so exquisitely beautiful. She looked up and saw Tim looking apprehensively at her.

"Please my darling," he said softly, "say you'll marry me, you must marry me. I know we have known each other only a short while but I feel we are soul mates. We must be together. Please, please say yes."

Jenny felt as if her heart would burst with happiness. It was true they hadn't know each other that long but it was long enough to know this was the man she wanted to spend her life with.

She found she had tears rolling down her face and she couldn't stop them, neither could she speak. She just looked at Tim and nodded.

Tim stood up and walked round the table. He pulled her up and into his arms and whispered, "I promise you I will spend the rest of my life making you as happy as you have me my wonderful Jenny."

Before Jenny had time to answer, there was a loud burst of applause and they both turned to see they had an audience of about a dozen people. Tim looked at Jenny with a grin from ear to ear.

"There you see, I have witnesses. Now you can't back out. I think this calls for champagne all round."

It was very late when Tim pulled his car up at Jenny's front door. Neither of them wanted the evening to come to an end. Tim had accepted Jenny's offer of coffee just to prolong the evening. Jenny turned the key in the lock and Tim followed her in.

Jenny was disappointed to find Ben wasn't in. She was bursting to tell him the news. They both sat down on the sofa and Tim put his arm around Jenny.

"I want you to come and spend the weekend at my parent's home darling. I can't wait to show you off to everyone."

Jenny sat up suddenly. She had been so happy that she had forgotten just who Tim was. Here was the man she had just promised to marry and he just happened to be her boss. Then there was the fact that he was worth a fortune. What would his parents think when he introduced her as his fiancée? What would her friend say? All at once she was afraid. They came from different worlds. Surely his family would not be pleased that their only son wanted to marry a girl that worked in one of their stores.

As if reading her mind, Tim pulled her close to him again. "Don't worry about a thing my love. Everything will be all right. They will love you when they meet you. Besides, my mother has been telling me for ages that it's time I was married."

Jenny once again sat up straight. She looked at the ring sparkling on her finger and without thinking began to twist it round and round.

"I can't meet them Tim, I'm scared. We come from different backgrounds. They won't want me to marry you, I know they won't. This is a mistake."

Tim stood up and pulled her up with him. He put his hand under her chin and said in a firm voice, "Now you listen to me Jenny. What we have decided tonight is final. Whatever happens I will marry you. I don't care how, where, when or whatever anyone says. We will be married. There is no power on this earth that will stop us. I love you with all my heart and I will be saying that to you when we are looking after our grandchildren. Now stop giving me a hard time and kiss me."

Jenny let herself be drawn into his arms again and gave herself up to the magic of his kiss.

Later when Tim had gone, Jenny sat looking in awe at her beautiful ring. She didn't have the confidence that Tim had. She felt there was trouble ahead but she had no idea just how much.

A few days later, Jenny was on her way to meet her future family. She had packed and unpacked her bag three times. Soon they had left the city behind and were driving through countryside that was bursting with the new life of spring. At any other time, Jenny would have been delighted with the scenery but not today.

Beside her, Tim was aware of how nervous she was. He had tried desperately to put her at ease but was fighting a losing battle. He pulled his car into the side of the road and switched off the engine. Picking up her hand he put it to his lips and kissed her fingers.

"Cheer up sweetheart. I promise they won't bite. This time next week you'll wonder why you were so worried." Jenny squeezed his fingers and gave him a smile.

"OK then, let's get it over with."

Tim reached over and gave her a peck on the cheek, switched on the ignition and they were back on their way.

Jenny got her first sight of Tim's country home half an hour later.

There was an avenue of trees leading up to the house. Under the trees were masses of daffodils. They reminded Jenny of the poem by William Wordsworth. She was enchanted. The house itself was enormous. It was three storeys high. At each end of the house there was an octagonal tower. These had been built in the fourteenth century. The materials used were flint and brick mixed. They reminded Jenny of a church. Over the front entrance, carved in the stonework was the heraldic shield of long dead ancestors of Tim's. Previous inhabitants of the house had rebuilt and remodelled it. Each leaving their stamp on the house. Despite all this, the house managed to retain a look of grandeur.

Tim helped her out of the car and they walked towards the house. He rang the bell and an elderly woman answered the door. At the sight of Tim, her face lit up. Tim bent down and gave her a kiss on the cheek. This had the effect of making her smile even wider.

"How are you Dora?" Tim asked, and without waiting for an answer he turned to Jenny and said, "This is Dora. She looked after me from the day I was born. I love her to bits. Dora, this is the lady I'm going to marry. Isn't she gorgeous?"

Dora turned to Jenny and gave her a smile. "It's a pleasure to meet you Miss. I hope you'll be very happy." Turning back to Tim she said, "Mr and Mrs Knight are in the drawing room sir."

Tim took Jenny by the hand and led her forward. Jenny took a deep breath and crossed the threshold.

Chapter Seven

The hall was large and welcoming. The highly polished floor echoed Jenny's feet as she walked. There was a sweeping staircase to the right. At each end of the staircase were small tables, filled with spring flowers set in delicate crystal bowls. To the left was another long table but Jenny had no time to take in any more of her surroundings as she was being whisked along by Tim.

By the time they reached the drawing room Jenny was quite out of breath. Tim stopped by the door and quickly took Jenny into his arms. He knew how nervous she was and he wanted to reassure her again. He gave her a lingering kiss, then reached for her hand again.

"Here we go," he joked and opened the door. His parents looked up as they entered.

As Jenny looked at Mr Knight she could see how Tim would look when he was in his fifties. They had the same build and the same blue eyes but instead of dark hair, Mr Knight's hair had turned white. It looked very distinguished. He stood up and Jenny saw he even had the same mannerisms as his son. He was dressed in a dark green cashmere sweater with dark green trousers. He held out his hand to Jenny and smiled.

"It's very nice to meet you my dear. I hope you had a pleasant journey. The countryside is so pleasant at this time of year don't you think?"

Jenny smiled back and shook his hand. "The journey was fine thank you and I agree with you, I think the spring is a lovely time of year."

Tim took her by the elbow and took her over to his mother. He bent down and kissed her on each cheek. "Mother this is my Jenny. My bride to be."

Jenny felt her face go red as she looked at Tim's mother. "I'm delighted to meet you Mrs Knight," said Jenny. All of a sudden Jenny wished she had not worn trousers. She felt uncomfortable as she looked at this elegant woman dressed in a lilac jumper and a dove grey skirt. The material was of the finest wool. Her shoes were the same shade as her jumper. Her eyes were blue but not the same shade as her son's. They seemed to take in everything about Jenny at one glance. Her hair was put up in a French plait. She looked immaculate. Just as Jenny had imagined she would.

For a moment she sat perfectly still. Then she slowly stood up and took both of Jenny's hands. She looked Jenny in the eyes and smiled.

"My dear you must call me Fiona. My goodness. What beautiful hair you have. The colour is glorious. Now let me see this engagement ring."

She lifted up Jenny's left hand and looked at the ring. Jenny was still feeling embarrassed. She wondered if Tim's mother would think the huge diamond was too extravagant. Fiona briefly looked at the ring and looking into Jenny's eyes said, "It's very nice dear but with those eyes I wonder if it should have been emeralds."

Jenny didn't know what to reply. She was saved from answering by the arrival of Dora. She was carrying a very large tray upon which was coffee and Tim's favourite fruitcake. She beamed at everyone and said to Tim, "I thought you would all be ready for this by now. I've made your favourite cake for you and I don't want to see any left mind."

Tim laughed at her and winked at Jenny. "She still thinks I'm ten years old but for a taste of her cake it's worth putting up with. Dora makes the best cake bar none."

Dora grinned from ear to ear and left the room.

They all sat down. Fiona picked up the silver coffee-pot and began to pour the coffee. After they had all finished and the cake had disappeared Jenny felt more relaxed. Fiona wasn't quite so frightening but Jenny was not sure about Mr Knight. It was as if he was summing her up and reserving judgement.

After a while Fiona looked at her watch. Turning to Tim and Jenny she said, "I hope you will forgive us but we have to pop out for a while. Try to relax this afternoon. Take Jenny for a walk Tim. Show her the stables."

Mr and Mrs Knight walked to the door. Fiona turned, as she was about to leave the room and looked at Tim. "I almost forgot to say darling. I hope you don't mind but I invited the Armstrong's to dinner tonight. I thought we should have a little celebration in honour of your engagement. I know Amanda is dying to meet Jenny."

With that she went. Tim was not very happy that they were to have Amanda and her parents over tonight. He had wanted it to be just the four of them so that they could get to know each other a little better. He sat down next to Jenny and pulled her into his arms. She snuggled against him, glad that they were on their own for a while.

"Sorry darling." he said. "I had expected a quiet dinner tonight but it seems Mother has other plans. Never mind. We have a lifetime of quiet dinners ahead of us."

*****

Amanda had been devastated when she learned that Tim had become engaged. For the first two days she had locked herself in her bedroom pretending she had a migraine. She had no idea who the girl was and where they had met. Amanda thought she knew all of Tim's friends. After the shock had worn off a little she had started to feel angry. She thought she had been made a fool of. Tim knew she loved him. Maybe this was just a passing fancy. Maybe Tim was doing it to keep his father quiet for a while. Yes that must be it. His father was always telling him it was about time he was married. That must be the reason. Tim was doing it to please his father and to get him off his back for a while. Later, he would break the engagement. She was sure that was it. There really was nothing to worry about. Meanwhile there was this tedious dinner party to get through.

She had taken great care to look her best. She wore a dress that had been especially designed for her in Paris. It was very low, very tight and very French. She wore her hair up because she knew how lovely the curve of her neck looked. Amanda was also aware that her eyes were her best feature, especially her long, thick eyelashes. She certainly knew how to use them. At the moment they were focused on Tim's father. He was handing her a drink. She smiled sweetly as she took the fine crystal glass from him. "Well, Uncle Toby, you are looking especially handsome tonight. Don't you think so Aunt Fiona?"

Fiona Knight just smiled and looked at her husband. She wasn't really in the mood for this tonight. She was still rather in shock over her son's engagement. To be honest she wasn't sure she was happy about it. She knew Toby was disappointed. He had wanted Amanda and Tim to marry. In fact they had all expected it. Fiona looked over at her oldest friend and her heart went out to her. She knew what a brave face Elizabeth was putting on. They had talked for years about the kind of wedding their children would have. They had even picked out names for their grandchildren. It would have been wonderful. They all knew how much Amanda loved Tim. Now the dream had gone.

Elizabeth was chatting away to her husband as if this was just another informal dinner. Fiona knew what an effort it was for her. She glanced up and saw Fiona watching her. The two women locked eyes for a moment. Each knew the others thoughts. They smiled sadly at each other and looked away.

Elizabeth's husband, however, was not bothering to hide his feelings. He was not interested in making small talk and wasn't going to bother trying. He drained his glass and held it out to Toby. "Time for another one I think before the happy couple show up."

Toby took his glass and went to refill it. He looked at his oldest friend and thought he looked as if he had had enough already. They were all a bit surprised about this engagement but it was no use drowning ones sorrows. He handed the glass to George Armstrong and watched as he tossed it back in one gulp.

Amanda stood up and walked over to the fireplace. She was just going to ask when they were going to meet the guest of honour when the door opened. In spite of her feelings, Amanda could see what a spectacular couple they looked. Tim looked so handsome she felt her heart break. Proudly he walked into the room with his fiancée on his arm. She wore a short black dress with long sleeves. Her hair was loosely tied back. Amanda stared at her hair. It was beautiful. She was looking up at Tim and Amanda saw him put his hand up and stroke her hair. She hated the girl on sight.

"Sorry to have kept you waiting everyone but I wanted to introduce Jenny to cook. I'm glad to say she approves."

The next few minutes were taking up with introductions. Giving Amanda time to study her rival. As soon as she had seen her, Amanda had the feeling they had met before. The feeling persisted while they went into dinner.

Jenny wasn't enjoying herself at all. As soon as she had seen Amanda she had wanted to turn and run. This was the woman in the store that had put lipstick on the gown. She had been so rude to Jenny.

Her mother and father were here also. Jenny had seen the frown on the older woman's face, as if she were trying to remember something. Jenny felt her face go red. She looked at the three women. So elegant and poised. Jenny felt awkward. She wished she had taken more time to dress. She was convinced she had made the wrong choice of dress. As if he could read her thoughts Tim squeezed her hand and Jenny instantly felt reassured.

Jenny was not really aware of what they were eating. She was, however, aware of everything else. She was a little overawed at the splendour of her surroundings. She felt she was out of her depth and she began to worry if she and Tim were not being too hasty. The meal was a misery for Jenny but there was even worse to come.

After dinner they all went back into the drawing room. Tim sat beside Jenny and held her hand. He knew she was feeling far from happy so he whispered in her ear, "Hold on a little bit longer darling. It's almost over." But her ordeal was just beginning.

Amanda took out a cigarette and lit it. She was determined to make Jenny squirm. She sat back in her chair and looked at Jenny. Her eyes were cold but her voice was so sweet. "Darling," she almost purred at Jenny, "I have been trying to think where I have seen you before. I have this ludicrous feeling that it was in the store. Surely I must be wrong."

Jenny knew her face was red yet again. She wanted to turn and run but she was powerless to do anything. She opened her mouth to speak but Tim got in first.

"No Amanda you are not wrong. Jenny and I did meet in the store. In fact I have you to thank for our getting together. If it wasn't for you we might never have met. We will be eternally grateful to you won't we Jenny?"

Amanda smiled sweetly at him and nodded her head. She was livid at Tim. When she realised that she had indeed brought these two together she felt sick with anger. She hadn't realised before that she had been responsible for wrecking her own happiness. What a fool she had been. Never mind they weren't married yet. She turned again to Jenny.

"Don't you think it will be a little difficult for you at work? I expect Tim will be a little embarrassed won't you Tim?"

Before anyone could answer, Toby Knight stood up. He took a deep breath and seemed to tower over them all as he answered in a not too quiet voice. "No, Tim will not be at all embarrassed because as from now Jenny no longer works at my store. In fact, Jenny no longer works full stop. We can't have our future daughter-in-law working can we Fiona. We have arranged to have a family meeting to discuss all the issues haven't we Jenny?"

Jenny was speechless. There was nothing she could say. She could hardly say this was the first she had heard of it. That would be calling her future father-in-law a liar. She was stunned by what he had just said. Now what was she supposed to do. She felt she had to get away. Taking all her courage she stood up. She looked at Fiona and said, "I do hope you will forgive me Mrs Knight but I have a bad headache and I would like to go to my room if I may. Thank you for a lovely evening."

Tim stood up. "Let me walk you upstairs darling."

The men stood up as Jenny and Tim left the room. Once outside Jenny just wanted to burst into tears. She felt totally humiliated. Tim closed the door and pulled her into his arms. He didn't know what to say to her. He was furious with his father for saying those things. The whole evening had been a disaster. Jenny had now been put in an embarrassing situation and he was dreadfully sorry for her. As for Amanda, he could quite cheerfully have strangled her.

He looked down at Jenny and could see her eyes were filled with unshed tears. "Pack you bags tonight darling. We will leave first thing in the morning."

Jenny looked up at him. She had never loved him more than this minute. He was trying to protect her. She drew a deep breath and pulling away from him said with dignity, "No Tim, I can't run away. There are things that have got to be sorted out. I was very surprised at what was said in there. If we leave in the morning things will only be made worse. We all need to talk."

Tom took her hand and they started to climb the stairs. Halfway up he stopped. "You're right Jenny. I was trying to avoid any unpleasantness but I can see now I was wrong. This is our future, yours and mine. We won't let people dictate to us how we live our lives. I will not allow my father to dictate to you. We must settle this."

"To be fair," said Jenny. "I can understand your father. It must have been a shock when you told your parents you were going to marry a girl from his store. I don't suppose I'm quite what they had in mind for you. Besides, they know nothing about me. For all they know I may only be interested in you for your money. After all you are their only son. The thing is though it looks as if I have lost my job now. I can see that it's bad for your image for me to work at the store. On the other hand I do need a job." She put her hand over Tim's mouth as he started to interrupt. "I can guess what you're going to say darling but I really do have to earn my own money."

"In that case Miss Woods," Tim said, "the sooner we get married and start a family the better Now let's put all of this behind us for now. I promised you once that nothing would ever come between us. That also goes for my parents and every one of their damn stores." He pulled her up and they continued up the stairs. When they kissed goodnight, all of their problems fell away from them.

Later, in bed Jenny couldn't sleep. She kept going over the events of the evening. She knew that she and Amanda Armstrong would never be friends. Her feminine intuition told her that Amanda was in love with Tim. She wondered if he knew. Both families seemed very close. Maybe Tim's father had wanted Tim and Amanda to marry.

Amanda certainly acted as if she had a right to be in this house. Jenny wondered if she would ever fit in. She got up and went to look out of the window. It was a full moon. From her window Jenny had a view of the garden. She looked at the shadows made by the garden statues. It looked so peaceful. She could see an enormous cedar tree. Its branches touched the ground. It looked as if it had been there forever and Jenny imagined Tim playing in it as a little boy. A smile came to her lips. She thought maybe one day they would have a son to play there as well. She realised she was cold so she got back into bed. The vision she had conjured up in her mind took away the worries of the evening and she fell asleep with a smile on her lips.

The rest of the weekend wasn't so bad as Jenny feared it would be. They had ended up having a meeting after all. It had been decided that Jenny would carry on working at the store after all. At least for a while. They had also decided to keep the engagement secret for the time being from the people at the store. Jenny needed time to prepare for the wedding. She had explained that she had no parents and she was determined to stand on her own two feet. She had stuck to her guns about working. In the end the Knights had come round to her way of thinking. At least they had for the moment. Tim's mother had secretly admired the way Jenny had stood up to her husband. It took guts. Mr Knight, however, thought differently.

Chapter Eight

The following months were the happiest of Jenny's life. She continued to work at the store and kept her engagement a secret from her fellow workers apart from Tina. Tina had been amazed at the news but true to her sweet nature had been delighted for her friend. She had drooled over Jenny's ring and thought it a pity that Jenny had to wear it on a chain around her neck while she was working. Tina had wanted Jenny to flaunt it at first but she understood why the engagement was a secret for the time being. Tina had met Tim socially and she had been very much in awe of him at first. However, Tim's natural charm had won her over and she had quickly become a firm fan of his.

She had teased Jenny and told her if she hadn't got her Bill she would have given Jenny some competition. Jenny was very happy that her dearest friend approved of her engagement. She was, however, sad because Tina had moved away. She had by now married her beloved Bill. Bill's aunt had died and as he was the only relative she had left, he had inherited her house in Devon. Now the newly weds were happily settled and running a bed and breakfast. Jenny really missed Tina, especially at work. They had been such good friends. Jenny had been a bridesmaid at the wedding. Tina had made a beautiful bride. When she had walked out of the church on the arm of her proud new husband, Jenny had wept. She wished Tim had been with her but he had been unable to be there. There was only one thing that had spoiled the day as far as Jenny was concerned. Richard had been best man.

They hadn't see each other since that dreadful day at the hospital. It had been excruciatingly embarrassing for both of them. They had managed to keep apart most of the time but when they couldn't avoid each other Jenny couldn't look him in the eye. Richard had been very polite and formal. Jenny was miserable about never being able to tell him the truth. Tina had told Richard about Jenny being engaged. Jenny had asked her to do so. Richard had stiffly congratulated her and wished her luck.

Her brother was also over the moon about it, although Jenny

secretly wondered if it was the fact that Tim had so much money that Ben liked so much. Whatever it was, Ben had been behaving himself lately. He had even stopped bringing Tony to the house, for which Jenny was eternally grateful.

She had almost succeeded in blotting out the past. Only on rare occasions did she still have nightmares where she would wake up in a panic, her heart racing. Then she would get up and pace the floor or sit up in bed hugging her knees to her chest. As time went by the horrendous images dragged up from her memory were gradually receding into the past.

There was so much going on in her life now. Jenny was still not quite at ease with Tim's father. She was by now used to spending weekends at Tim's parents and whilst she felt she was making headway with Mrs Knight, there was still some reserve between herself and Toby Knight. He still resented Jenny working. Jenny, however, still had no intentions of giving up just yet.

Mrs Jenkins had recently retired and she had recommended Jenny taking over as head of the department. This suggestion had been taken and Jenny was now promoted. This had also meant a substantial rise in pay that meant Jenny could put more away each month toward her wedding.

Tim was sensitive to Jenny's needs. He knew how important it was for her to be independent and he was touched by it. He would have liked nothing more than to give her everything she desired but he knew she would always have to be her own person and he loved her even more for it. He would often think of the difference between Jenny and Amanda. Life with Amanda would have been one long round of parties and shopping. Still to be fair to Amanda, she had acted better than Tim thought she would at the news of his engagement. She had even been friendly to Jenny. Tim really thought Amanda had grown to like Jenny.

As far as Amanda was concerned, Tim was still very naïve. Amanda's feelings for Jenny were the same as they had always been. She hated her with a passion born of envy. She would never give up the idea that one day Tim would want her. In the meantime she would tolerate that little shop girl.

Jenny was fully aware of Amanda's feeling towards her. She had known from the start that Amanda was in love with Tim. At times she could almost feel sorry for her but then she would be on the receiving end of one of Amanda's jibes. Then she would once again make allowances; she could afford to overlook petty remarks because she was the one that had Tim's love, not Amanda. Jenny was the only one that wasn't fooled by Amanda's show of friendship. The others didn't notice the coldness in her eyes as she smiled at Jenny. Nor did they notice how there was always an invitation to do things that Jenny had no interest in whatever. For instance, Jenny hated horses. She was afraid of them and had no inclination to ride whatever.

When Amanda had found this out she did her utmost to get Jenny out riding. She had even suggested to Tim that he buy Jenny a horse so that they could all ride together.

Tim had thought this a wonderful idea and had immediately bought the most beautiful horse. With the help of Amanda he had bought a complete riding outfit for Jenny.

On their next visit to Tim's parent he had excitedly taken her down to the stables, telling Jenny he had a surprise for her.

Jenny was horrified when Amanda led out of the stable an enormous horse. It was prancing and rearing about and Jenny almost fainted with fright when Amanda put the reins into Jenny's hands. She smiled sweetly at Jenny, knowing exactly how scared Jenny was.

With a cry of panic Jenny dropped the reins and spinning around ran off.

Tim immediately chased after her and catching her up pulled her into his arms and held her close until she had stopped trembling. Tim had explained that he had wanted to give her the horse as a surprise. Jenny had to confess how she felt about horses. In the end they had both laughed about it and the horse had gone back.

Amanda had pretended to be concerned for Jenny and had offered to teach her to ride.

Tim had quite firmly told her that it would not be necessary as he intended to give up riding as Jenny hated it so much.

Amanda was furious with this news. She loved to ride with Tim. It was one of her favourite things. Now that little shop girl had taken something else away from her. One day she would make her pay in full for all the hurt and humiliation she was feeling. Amanda as yet didn't know just how she was going to bring about the downfall of that little upstart but she was determined she would.

Chapter Nine

Richard looked down at the woman held in his arms. She was lovely. As they danced around the floor he kissed the top of her head. She looked up into his face and smiled. His arm tightened around her waist and he closed his eyes, giving himself up to the music and the feeling of holding a beautiful woman again. He breathed in her perfume. At last he was beginning to feel alive again. Ever since that day he had taken Jenny into the hospital when his whole world had fallen apart he had felt dead inside.

He had carried on doing his job because there was nothing left to do. The hospital was all there was left to him now. It was strange really. The hospital was where his life had been ripped apart and where it had started again. He thought of the day this woman he was holding had walked into his life. She had injured her wrist. It had not been broken after all. She had been very pleased with the news; she had also been very pleased with the handsome young doctor. She had made no bones about going all out for him.

Richard had been very flattered and when she had pursued him outside of the hospital, he had finally succumbed. They had been out together a few times since then. Now Richard was her partner at a birthday party of one of her friends.

To begin with the evening had started out as a bit of a shock to Richard. When he had found out who's birthday they were celebrating he had wanted to leave at once. He had been rooted to the spot when Amanda had pointed out their host. She had linked her arm in his and pulled him through the crowd. He had found himself looking at Tim Knight and there on his arm was Jenny looking radiant. The smile had frozen on her face as she saw him.

Amanda, however, seemed not to notice and had introduced Richard. She had smiled up at Tim and said, "This is my divine doctor, isn't he handsome?"

Tim had put out his hand and Richard found himself shaking it and looking into his face. He was surprised to find he couldn't feel any animosity toward Tim.

Jenny was standing very still as if she wanted to be invisible. Richard had shaken her hand and she had nodded but not spoken.

Amanda had noticed something going on between Jenny and Richard. She felt instinctively there was tension between them. Maybe there was something she could use at last. She enjoyed Richard's company. He was fun to be with and he was very good looking but there was only one man for her. She linked her arm through Richard's and said, "It's about time we had another drink darling. See you later birthday boy." With that she turned Richard around and they walked away.

Jenny watched them go with a feeling of relief. She had heard Amanda had a boyfriend but it was a shock to discover it was Richard. She hadn't expected to ever seen him again after Tina's wedding. She became aware that Tim was talking to her. She smiled up at him. "Sorry sweetheart I was miles away. What did you say?"

Tim picked up her hand and kissed it. "I was saying my beautiful one, I can see my mother frantically trying to get my attention. If you will excuse me I will be right back."

Jenny watched him walk over to where his mother was, then she turned and walked out onto the terrace.

The evening had started out so well. Tim's parents had organised a surprise party for Tim. Jenny had been in on it and it had made her feel as if she had at last been accepted. The last person she had expected to see with Amanda was Richard. She walked over to the wall at the edge of the terrace. It was lovely and cool here. The scent of flowers wafted up at her. She leaned her elbows on the wall and gazed out into the darkness. From here she could just make out the big cedar tree. For some reason that tree had become a favourite with Jenny. She remembered the first night she had stayed in this house and how she had imagined her children playing in it. It would be wonderful when she and Tim were married. Tim had been pressing her to name the day very soon and Jenny had decided to tell him tonight that she wanted to marry him at the end of the year.

Jenny became aware of somebody behind her. Thinking it was Tim she turned with a smile on her lips. With a shock she saw it was Richard standing before her with two glasses of champagne in his hands. He looked as surprised as she did. He clearly felt embarrassed and shifted from one foot to the other.

"Sorry if I startled you," he said, "I thought I saw Amanda come out here."

Jenny shook her head. They stood looking at one another now knowing what to say. Richard was the first to break the silence.

"Look here," he said, "this is stupid. We have known each other long enough, surely we can at least be civil to each other, especially if we are destined to keep meeting. Why don't you take one of these drinks and we will drink to the past and the future."

Jenny felt the tears fill her eyes but she was pleased and touched by Richard's words. She reached out and took a glass from him and raised it. "I can think of nothing nicer Richard," she said softly.

They both sipped their champagne. Richard looked at Jenny and thought how lovely she was and how much he still loved her. He had resigned himself to the fact that he would always love her. There was one thing that had tortured him through all of those lonely months. He had paced the floor night after night. Now he could hold back no longer. He had to ask, he had a right to know.

Summing up his courage he looked down at Jenny. Taking a deep breath he said, "Jenny, I must ask you this. I promise I will never speak of it again but I must know. Who was the father of the baby?"

Jenny's legs turned to jelly. She thought she was going to fall so she sat down on the edge of the wall. A hundred thoughts flashed into her mind but she couldn't speak. At last she was able to find her voice. She still felt the pain of what Richard thought was a betrayal of his love but she must keep it to herself forever. She looked up at him and gently touched his arm.

"Richard I can't tell you who the father was. Believe me it's better left. I really didn't know I was pregnant or I would have told you myself. Please, please do not speak of it again. I will always be sorry for what you went through but I did suffer myself. Even now I still wake up in the night and think about it. I don't think it will ever go away completely. I love Tim with all my heart and I want to marry him and start a new life. We must both put it behind us or it will destroy us. Please Richard for the sake of what we once meant to each other. Tell me you forgive me and let's move on."

Richard looked down at the woman who was his whole life. He saw the pain on her face and his heart once again ruled his head. He kissed her gently on the cheek and said with a voice full of emotion, "Oh Jenny, when could I ever deny you anything? If that's what it takes to make you happy then I forgive you." He took the empty glass from her hand and walked away.

Jenny gave a sigh and then she jumped as she heard a movement to her right. With a start she realised there was somebody there. Then she almost fell backwards as she saw a cigarette lighter burst into flame and the light illuminated a face. It was the last person in the world Jenny wanted to overhear the conversation she had just had. She felt as if she had been turned to ice as she watched the smoke from the cigarette spiral upwards and Amanda slowly stand up and walk to her.

"Well now. Shall you tell Tim or will I?"

Jenny was unable to move. She was in complete shock. To think that Amanda, of all people had found out her dreadful secret. There was no way she would keep quiet about it. Jenny knew Amanda hated her. Now she had all she needed to hurt her in the worst possible way. Jenny gave a sob and buried her face in her hands. The moonlight glinted on the ring on Jenny's finger and the flash of brilliance drove Amanda into action.

She sprang at Jenny and pulled at her hand. With a triumphant snarl she sneered, "Let me return this to Tim for you. I don't think you will have the courage to do it yourself will you. It's all over now wouldn't you say?" As she was speaking she was tearing the ring off Jenny's finger. Amanda was almost beside herself with happiness but she wasn't finished yet. She put her face up close to Jenny, "Get out," she said. "I will give you half an hour to pack your bags and go. Don't even think of saying goodbye to Tim. When he finds out what a little tramp you are he will realise what a lucky escape he's had. Now go."

She watched in pure delight as Jenny ran off into the darkness. Amanda held up the diamond ring and smiled at the rainbow of colours glinting in the moonlight. She slipped it onto her finger and held her hand up admiring it. Yes it was a pretty enough ring but give Tim a little time to get over that little whore and she would have a ring on her finger that would make this one look as if it came from Woolworth's.

Meanwhile she wanted to have a word with Doctor Richard Evans.

She took the ring off her finger and put it in her pocket, then with a smile on her face she turned and headed for the ballroom. She felt as if she were walking on air.

Chapter Ten

The sea was deep blue and very calm. It stretched on forever. The whole world was water and sun. The man at the helm of the thirty-two foot cruising yacht lifted his head and stared out to the horizon. Not even a seagull intruded into this other world of peace and tranquillity. He looked down at the water and watched the wake from the boat as it sliced through the water. Out here, away from everything, he could almost forget. How was it possible to go from feeling so alive and blissfully happy one minute, then feeling dead inside the next? He actually groaned out loud as despite himself his thoughts returned to that awful night of his birthday party. He was filled with conflicting emotions, sorrow and bitterness. Most of all he was angry with Amanda.

It was she that had given him the awful details of Jenny's past. She had been bubbling over with glee. She had tried hard to hide the triumph she was feeling but it was obvious to Tim that she gloried in the telling. Her eyes had sparkled as she told Tim about the baby Jenny had been expecting and how she had an abortion because she didn't want to be encumbered with a baby. After the first shock, his first impulse had been to take her lovely neck into his hands and squeeze it until she could no longer besmirch his lovely Jenny. Instead he had taken the ring that she had held out to him and put it in his pocket.

Amanda had put her arms around his neck and made what she thought were comforting noises. Tim had reached up and extricated himself from her grasp. He was white to the lips. Surely this wasn't true. Amanda must be making this up. She was always trying to cause trouble between him and Jenny. Then he realised that even Amanda wouldn't go that far. There must be something he didn't know about. He decided he wouldn't take anyone's stories. He would find his beloved Jenny and she would tell him the truth. She was far too honest to deceive him. He would trust her with his life.

He had suddenly felt ashamed for doubting her. He would go to her now and they would laugh at Amanda's latest effort to spoil things for them. Then he would slip the ring back on Jenny's finger and they would dance the night away. However, there was no more dancing for Tim that night. Jenny was nowhere to be seen. He eventually discovered that Jenny had packed her bags and left.

At first he couldn't believe it but as time went on there was no word from Jenny. Even her brother could or would not help him.

Tim was alone. There was nothing in the world that could make him feel better. He could not imagine his life without Jenny now. Everything was pointless. He was just going through the motions of living. At last he could stand it no longer and had decided to take off on his own for a while. He hadn't been on his yacht for some time now. Tim was a competent sailor. He had spent most of his teenage years on the water. He had been meaning to introduce Jenny to the pleasures of cruising but now that would never happen.

With a start Tim realised there were tears on his cheeks. He lifted his hand and brushed them away. He shook his head as if to shake off the thoughts that were flooding his memory. He must concentrate on himself and the sea. Out here things were put into perspective. Things could change in a matter of minutes. Man was no match for the ever-changing sea.

At the moment, the ocean was calm but there was a breeze getting up and Tim was well aware that anytime that cooling breeze could become a raging force strong enough to toss his yacht and reduce it to matchwood.

For the moment, the day was tranquil and as beautiful as an oil painting.

Tim reached into his pocket and pulled out the ring Jenny had worn so proudly on her finger. He held it up to the sun and the diamond exploded into a myriad of colour. Tim was mesmerised by it beauty. He remembered the look on Jenny's face when he had put it on her finger. The look in her eyes as she held it up was almost one of reverence. He remembered the way her beautiful hair had shone in the light from the fire. In his mind he heard once again his voice say to Jenny as he held her on that memorable night, "I promise you I will spend the rest of my life making you as happy as you have made me my wonderful Jenny."

Tim put the ring to his lips and kissed it. Then with all his might he threw the ring into the ocean. He saw one last flash of its brilliance as it fell. Lost forever, gone, and Tim felt it had taken his very soul with it.

He had been unaware of time slipping away until he realised it was getting dark. The wind had become much stronger and he was cold. He decided he would alter course and head toward land. The weather had taken a turn for the worse so he lashed the tiller and took the main sail down and then he went below to change into some warm clothes. He made himself a hot drink, which lifted his spirits a little.

Returning up on deck he was glad he now had oilskins on as the rain had started and it looked as if it was going to be quite a night. Tim wasn't unduly concerned. He hoisted the storm jib and took in the jib sail. Two hours later, the weather worsened. He switched on the engine and resigned himself to a long cold night.

Despite the wind howling and the rain blowing horizontally at times, Tim almost found solace. Out here alone battling with the elements he had to concentrate fully all of the time. Darkness was all around him now. The wind didn't let up. It was if anything louder, as if all the lost souls from the deep were bewailing their fate. Halfway through the night, Tim began to feel very tired. He wondered what it would be like to just give up and slip over the side to join the countless unfortunate dead in their watery graves.

Eventually, the blackness started to give way to the new day. The rain at last stopped and the wind abated a little. Tim was able to get his first view of land ahead. The sky was still threatening and the waves were still angry as Tim at last came within the safety of the harbour.

An old man had been watching Tim's progress as he had battled against the elements for the last hour. He knew what it was to be cold and wet and completely exhausted out alone on the sea. He was too old now to go out alone but he still hankered after the time when he was at one with the ocean.

As Tim came alongside the harbour wall the old man made ready to catch the rope.

Tim threw the rope and the old man not having lost any of his old skills, deftly caught it. He made fast the rope and stood back watching Tim as he prepared to jump ashore to adjust it.

That was when it happened. Tim started to jump at the same time a wave threw the boat up in the air. Tim found himself flailing about in mid-air. His arms desperately trying to reach the safety of the moorings. In a split second the boat was under him again and as his feet touched the deck his ankle snapped under him, his head hit the tiller and he was knocked unconscious.

Chapter Eleven

Toby and Fiona Knight stood at the bedside of their only son. He looked as if he would wake up any minute now. The bruise on his forehead had almost gone; there was just a trace of purple visible. His leg was in a cast but apart from that Tim looked healthy. Fiona turned from the bed and busied herself with the arrangements of flowers on the bedside table. Toby stood with shoulders slumped staring down at the young man in the bed.

Fiona looked at her husband. She thought how he had aged since that dreadful night when the telephone had awakened them from their sleep into a living nightmare. She went over and slipped her arm in his.

"I think he looks better today darling. Remember the doctors said he might be able to hear us so don't let him sense that your worried."

Toby gave her hand a squeeze. What would he do without this woman? He leaned over his son and brushed his hair with his hand. "Well old chap we'll be off now. See you tomorrow."

Fiona gave Tim a kiss and touched his cheek. "See you tomorrow darling," she whispered. They both looked back when they reached the door. He looked as if he were taking a nap and at any minute would sit up and wave to them. Except that he couldn't. He had been lying there for three weeks now.

The doctors had said there was no way of telling how long Tim would remain in a coma.

Everyone tried to be positive and would sit by Tim's bedside and talk to him for hours. At first his parents had refused to leave his side. They didn't want to miss being there when Tim opened his eyes. Then, as time went on and there was no change, they had allowed others to take over the vigil enabling them to get some rest.

Amanda had been with Tim every day. She would sit by his bedside and hold his hand, all the while talking to him. Had they allowed it, she would have stayed with him every night. Each day she would will him to open his eyes and look at her. As the weeks went by it was Amanda that looked ill. Not the man lying in the hospital bed.

Each day Amanda prayed this would be the day when Tim opened his eyes. She would tell him of the plans she had for their future together. She was convinced that Tim would be hers now that Jenny wasn't on the scene anymore.

Amanda had come to believe in the lies she had told Tim about Jenny. She still hated her with every fibre in her being. Once when she was sitting with Tim a nurse had come into his room. Under the cap that she wore was the same glorious colour hair as Jenny's. Amanda had almost physically thrown her out. She was more and more possessive of Tim.

It was Sunday morning and the room was particularly quiet. Tim's father was sitting in an armchair in the corner of the room reading the paper. His mother was yet again arranging more flowers. Amanda was as usual sitting by the bedside holding Tim's hand. The only noise in the room was the occasional rustle of the paper as Toby turned the page. The sun was shining through the window and it was pleasantly warm and peaceful. Amanda had her eyes closed and felt herself drifting off into a wonderful calm world where worries didn't exist.

All at once she was wide awake. She was so shocked that she gasped out loud. Tim's mother turned from her flower arranging and Toby Knight lowered his paper. Amanda leaped out of her chair and sent it flying backwards.

"He squeezed my hand," she cried. The colour drained from the face of Fiona as she looked at her beloved son. As she did so to her intense joy, he opened his eyes.

That had been the start of yet another nightmare for all of them. The euphoria they had felt when Tim had opened his eyes quickly turned to horror when it was discovered that Tim had completely lost his memory. He didn't even recognise his parents at first but as the months dragged on he started to remember things concerning his parents and himself. Unfortunately that's where it ended. Everything was a blank as far as Tim was concerned. He would get the most horrendous headaches and depression that could sometimes last for days. At times he would prowl around the grounds of his parent's home or just sit under the cedar tree and stare into space. The doctors had told him not to try and force his memory to come back. They said it might start to return at any time. To Tim this was so frustrating.

There was no way he could not try to remember. Always there was a feeling of urgency in his head. There was something that he wanted to do. He knew there was but there was no way he could remember. If he tried too hard to remember the pain would overwhelm him and he would once again sink down into despair.

It was far easier to give himself up to the delightful company of the young woman that was almost always at his side. Strange that he couldn't remember her. He was told they had always know each other. She was certainly a lovely young lady and Tim felt more at ease in her company than anyone's at the moment. Amanda was good for him in every way. She never tired to being with him and Tim was grateful for the care she lavished on him. For instance, Tim was not able to tolerate seeing his old friends just yet. He found it upsetting to be in the company of people at present. Apart from his parents and Amanda. It was Amanda that made sure he was left in peace. She let it be known that Tim would not be on the social scene for the foreseeable future.

Together they would ride or swim or sit in chairs on the lawn and listen to music. As time went by, Tim became more and more reliant on Amanda. She was almost a shield from the world. Both sets of parents found themselves holding their breath. Maybe, just maybe this would be the beginning of what they had hoped for.

As far as Amanda was concerned life just couldn't be better. It was wonderful to have Tim all to herself most of the time. The fact that he didn't remember her was a bonus to Amanda. She could make herself indispensable to him. He would fall in love with her now She knew it. There was no trace of that little shop girl in his memory. If at times she got afraid when Tim would try to remember, she could always divert him. It wasn't in her interest for Tim to regain his memory. What good would it do anyway? They were happy together now. This was how it was meant to be. Amanda had waited too long to be this close to Tim. Nothing and nobody was going to come between them again. She would make sure of it.

The summer came to an end and autumn faded into winter. Christmas was a very quiet time that year. Amanda and her parents were the only guests at the festivities in the Knights household. It was by now accepted by all that Tim would never fully regain his memory.

Tim was reconciled to the fact. He had started to come to terms with it but there were times, especially in the middle of the night, when he was racked with a feeling of such melancholy that he gave way to tears. He told no one of the intensity of his feelings. He didn't know what it was that stopped him from feeling really happy. He just knew deep down in his subconscious, something was stopping him from getting on with the rest of his life.

Chapter Twelve

The tears were streaming down her face as she ran blindly down the drive. Jenny hadn't even gone up to her room to pack. She had run out of the house through the servant's door. There were two maids working in the kitchen as Jenny had run through. They had stared at her with open mouths. Jenny hadn't even seen them.

She could still hear Amanda's voice in her head. She could still feel her hand hurting where Amanda had torn her beautiful ring from her finger. Two words were going round and round in her head. Its over, it's over and she wanted to die.

She knew Amanda would have gone straight to Tim and told him what she had overheard. She also knew that Amanda would embellish it. What chance had she now? Tim would hate her by the time Amanda had finished. What Amanda didn't know she would make up Jenny was sure of that. Except she would make up vicious lies about her, and Tim would never know they were lies. Why hadn't she told Tim herself? He had loved her so much he would have understood. Now it was too late.

She tripped over a pothole and went sprawling headlong into the dust. She picked herself up and carried on running. She felt the trickle of warm blood run down her leg. She had gashed her knee but was oblivious to the pain. Her shoe had come off but she ran on heedlessly. All that was in her mind now was to get away.

At first she was unaware of the car behind her. Then she realised somebody was calling her name. With a surge of happiness she thought Tim had come after her. She stopped running and stood waiting to be held in his embrace once again. To her utter dismay she saw not Tim get out of the car but Richard. All her hopes were dashed again. With a little moan she slumped to the ground unconscious.

Richard picked her up gently and laid her on the back seat. Jenny opened her eyes and looked up to see Richard's anxious face leaning over her. She sat up and put her hand up to her tangled hair. Richard caught her hand and held it tight.

"How are you feeling now dear?" he asked.

Jenny just stared at him as if he were speaking another language. She looked so hurt and lost. Richard wanted to sweep her into his arms but he didn't dare. She didn't respond to any of his questions. She sat upright staring straight ahead.

Richard put his coat round her shoulders and gently led her to the car. Moments later he was driving away.

There was no noise coming from the back at all. He glanced in the mirror and saw her still sitting bolt upright. With the moonlight streaming through the car window, she looked as if she were a beautiful statue. He decided she was suffering from shock and the best thing would be to get her home as quickly as possible.

A little later she seemed to relax. Her head fell forward and from sheer exhaustion, fell into a deep sleep.

When Jenny opened her eyes the sun was up. The events of the previous night came rushing back. She sat up straight and looking up saw Richard watching her in the driving mirror. She realised they had arrived at her house. Richard switched off the engine and sat very still. Jenny felt cold and tired, she discovered she hadn't even got her bag with her. She remembered how she had left everything at Tim's house. She looked at Richard and as if he could read her mind he turned to her saying, "Don't worry about a thing. All we have to do is bang on the door and Ben will let us in."

Ben opened the door still half asleep until he saw his sister. He stared open mouthed at the state Jenny was in. Richard didn't bother to explain until he had made Jenny a hot cup of tea. Then he told Ben only that there had been an argument and Jenny had split up with Tim. Ben was a bit upset with this news as he had plans for his own future that had counted on Tim's money. He wasn't very sympathetic with Jenny but he tried to hide his feelings.

Jenny had started to look better after her second cup of tea.

Richard was not happy about the way Jenny was behaving. He gently persuaded her to go and have a hot bath and to pack a bag. He had no intentions of leaving her in the state she was in. He didn't ask, he told Jenny and Ben that Jenny was going to stay with him for a while.

Ben seemed relieved at this.

As for Jenny, she seemed incapable of thinking for herself. For once Richard didn't give a damn about convention. If people would gossip over them so be it.

Ben did manage to cook them breakfast. Although Jenny just pushed hers around her plate. There was more colour in her cheeks now but she still wasn't talking. She hadn't said a word since last night.

Richard stood up and went to get Jenny's coat. He had put it over her shoulders and picked up her suitcase. "Don't worry about her," he said over his shoulder to Ben. "Things will be fine in a day or two."

For the first time Ben felt a surge of sympathy for his sister. She looked like a zombie standing there staring ahead. He went to her and gave her a hug.

"Don't worry sis," he said stroking her hair. "Things will sort themselves out."

She made no response and Richard gently opened the door and took her out to his car.

For the next two weeks Richard did his best to get Jenny back to normal. He had managed to take some time off work but was due back in a couple of days. He was worried about Jenny. He didn't want her to be left on her own so he made a phone call to Tina and Bill.

Tina was devastated when Richard told her what had happened. She and her husband insisted that Richard bring Jenny down to stay with them. It was a load off Richard's mind.

Being with her best friend once again seemed to help Jenny a great deal. Richard felt he could leave Jenny with Tina knowing she was in good hands. Still it was with apprehension he said goodbye and went back to work promising he would be back at every opportunity.

It was a month before he was able to spend time with them again. Jenny was looking a lot better. She was happy to see Richard again but there was no light in her eyes any more. She had become much thinner and had taken to wandering the Devonshire countryside alone.

As time went by Jenny started to help out with the guests. The bed and breakfast seemed to be doing well. After a while she became indispensable to Tina and Bill.

Tina was pregnant and she was not having an easy pregnancy. Jenny found herself more and more helping out with the guests. It was so different from her usual life. Jenny found she didn't get much time to herself. People were always coming and going. Sometimes she would fall into bed and through sheer exhaustion immediately fall asleep.

As autumn turned to winter visitors stopped coming. Jenny had more time on her hands. Although she missed seeing her brother, she had no desire to go back to the city. She had grown to love Devon as much as Tina and Bill did. When the snow came Jenny found solace in walking the fields. She felt she almost belonged out there alone. It was fitting, the snow covered everything. As nature had put everything into suspended animation so Jenny felt her heart had shut down. Inside she was as lonely as her one set of footprints in the snow. Tim still filled her every waking thought.

Christmas had been particularly bad for Jenny. Ben and Richard had come to join in the festivities. Everyone had enjoyed Christmas dinner. Tina wasn't allowed to do any cooking. Bill had insisted she put her feet up and rest while the men did the work. Things seemed fine. Jenny had put on an act that had fooled Ben but not the others. There had been a smile on her face most of the day but that night she had sobbed into her pillow. She remembered how she had hoped to be married at Christmas.

The spring came and Tina gave birth to a boy. Bill was so proud and happy. When Tina came home from the hospital Bill fussed around her like a mother hen. They decided to name the baby Danny. He was a beautiful little boy. He had his mother's looks and his father's sunny nature. He completely changed the life of the whole household. Jenny adored him. From the moment he arrived Danny had taken over. He had melted a place in Jenny's heart that had been frozen.

It was a hot summer afternoon in August. Tina, Bill and Jenny were taking a well-earned break. They were sitting on the lawn drinking a glass of wine. Danny was lying on a blanket on the grass. He had just found his toes and was delighted with himself.

Tina watched Jenny laughing at the antics of her son. She was glad that Jenny seemed more like her old self lately but wished Jenny would start to have a social life again. Jenny had plenty of offers from men to go out but she was just not interested. Tina knew that Jenny was still in love with Tim. There was nothing Tina could do to help her friend. It broke her heart to see Jenny suffer. She wondered once again if Bill had been right about not telling Jenny about Tim's accident.

They had seen the report in the paper how the son of a famous millionaire had suffered a dreadful accident. Bill had insisted that it would do Jenny no good to know about it because of her state of mind. So they had hidden the news from her. Tina now worried if they should have told her. Later there had been reports that Tim had lost his memory. This had convinced Bill that they had done the right thing but Tina wasn't so sure. She leaned over and took the newspaper away from Bill.

"I think we all deserve a treat because we have been working so hard. I propose that we close the B and B next weekend and go away for the weekend. All those in favour put your hand up."

Jenny immediately put her hand up. Bill slowly stretched his arms above his head and yawned. "What brought this on?" he asked

"As I just said," Tina replied, "we have all worked hard so I think it would be nice to have a break."

Bill began to look interested. "And have you thought where we should go," he asked smiling.

Tina nodded. "I think we should go to Salcombe. Remember we spent a week there Bill? I think Jenny would love it, especially watching the sailing boats competing. What do you say Jenny?"

Jenny nodded. "I think it's a wonderful idea."

Bill looked at the two women and shrugged. "If you both think it's a good idea then what chance do I have? I agree."

Tina jumped to her feet and picked the baby up. She swung him round and he laughed with delight. "Well master Danny we are going to see the sea. This will be your first holiday. Next year you will be old enough to build a sandcastle with Daddy."

Bill looked at Jenny and winked. "I was thinking that next year Danny may be able to play with a little sister."

Tina stood still and stared at Bill. "Now there's a thought," she said.

Chapter Thirteen

Everyone agreed that Tina had been right to suggest a break. The weather was glorious and they were all having fun. Jenny was feeling more relaxed than she had in months. She was looking beautiful in a dress of the palest green. Her skin was lightly tanned and the sunshine painted glorious colours in her hair. She was unaware that as every male passed her he would turn and stare.

Jenny was coming out of a shop with three ice creams in her hand. She paused at the top of the steps to look for her friends. She spotted them and was about to join them when she froze.

Danny had thrown a toy out of his pushchair. A man was stooping to pick it up for him. Everything seemed to go into slow motion for Jenny. She watched mesmerised as the man gave Tina Danny's toy. Tina seemed as if she were in a trance as she stood staring at the man before her. He smiled at her and looking down at Danny ruffled his hair. Then he was pulled away by the smartly dressed woman on his arm and they were soon lost in the crowd.

Bill and Tina stared after him. Neither one of them could speak. They were both totally shocked with the unexpected encounter. They had known who it was instantly but there had been not a flicker of recognition in the eyes of Tim Knight.

Tina was the first to move. She looked over to her friend and saw her standing in the shop doorway. Her heart went out to Jenny. She gave the pushchair to Bill and went over. There was no colour in Jenny's face. As Tina drew near she saw Jenny drop the ice cream and stagger back into the shop.

Tina went to Jenny and taking her by the hand led her out of the shop. Her fingers were like ice. Her eyes searched the crowds for another glimpse of him. Jenny felt her heart pounding; her legs were threatening to collapse under her. She wanted desperately to catch another glimpse of him but at the same time she wanted to run and hide. She wanted to be alone and relive seeing that beloved face once again. After months of longing for the sight of him he had reappeared for a fleeting second. It was too much to bear. She felt as if she were back once again to that night when her world had crashed around her. The irony of it was, the woman that had instigated the whole thing was by Tim's side now. Jenny saw again in her mind the way Amanda Armstrong had clung onto Tim's arm, as if she had claimed him.

She became aware that Tina was speaking to her. Jenny turned to face her and asked, "Why didn't he speak? I could understand him not talking to me but what have you done. Why did he just walk away as if he didn't know you."

Tina looked at Bill. "I think it's about time we told Jenny the whole truth."

Turning to Jenny she took her hand and said gently, "Jenny there's something we didn't tell you about Tim. I know now that we should have told you at the time but we wanted to stop you from being hurt again. Let's go back to the hotel and we will tell you everything."

Slowly they all made their way back. The day had been ruined. Each was lost in thought. Bill was thinking what rotten luck to run into Tim of all people.

Tina was wondering how Jenny would take the news of Tim's loss of memory.

And Jenny was still seeing his face.

*****

Amanda was feeling angry. Who would have dreamed they would bump into those people? She had seen the girl in the shop doorway. She had stood out with that ridiculous colour hair. Amanda would know her anywhere. Still Tim had no idea how close he had come with his past. What if he had seen her? Would he have remembered anything? There was always a chance that Tim could regain his memory. Why had she agreed to come with Tim to Salcombe?

Amanda was surprised that Tim still had an interest in boats after his accident. He still liked to sail at times and he had wanted to come down for a sailing weekend.

Amanda always jumped at the chance to have Tim all to herself so she had happily agreed to accompany him.

Things had been going very well for Amanda. Tim seemed happy to be in her company now more than ever before. Friends had started to treat them as a couple. Amanda thought it was just a matter of time now before they really were. The last thing she needed was for Jenny Woods to turn up. As luck would have it Tim hadn't seen her. It had been a shock for Amanda when they had come face to face with that ex-shopgirl though. She had held her breath when Tim had picked up that child's toy.

Amanda brought her thoughts back to the present and looked up to see Tim walking towards her with a drink in each hand. They were in the hotel bar, having a drink before going in to dinner.

Tim sat down opposite her. She took a sip of her gin and tonic and placed the glass on the table. Maybe now was the time to put into words what she had been meaning to say to Tim for months. Picking up his hand that had been resting on the table, she looked into his eyes and said, "Darling are you happy?" Without waiting for a reply she went on, "I wish you could remember how things were between us before your accident. I think I owe it to you to tell you that we were just about to announce out engagement. Perhaps it's selfish of me to tell you now but I find it so hard being with you and not being able to tell you how much I love you. Darling it's been hell. We were always together. Our love meant everything to me and now it's as if it never happened. I don't know how much longer I can go on like this."

She managed to make tears come to her eyes. She let go of Tim's hand and taking out a handkerchief, gently dabbed her eyes making sure that she didn't spoil her mascara. Her heart was pounding. Was she doing the right thing? On the other hand, what had she got to lose? She was tired of waiting around for Tim to make a move. Might as well go for it.

She stole a look at Tim. He was staring wide-eyed at her. For one heart stopping moment she thought she had blown her chances. He looked amazed at what she had just said. Then he gently took her hand and held it in both of his.

"Dearest Amanda, I'm so sorry. You must think I'm a blind fool. I had no idea. It must have been a nightmare for you. To think all this time you have been helping me get my life back together and I didn't notice how unhappy you are because of me. How could I have been so selfish?"

Amanda managed a weak smile. "Don't blame yourself. It's not your fault. Still now you know the situation, where do we go from here?"

Tim gave a great sigh and leaned back in his chair. "Please understand Amanda. I do care for you very much. Any man would be a fool not too. You are a very beautiful woman. I would like nothing more than to settle down, raise a family and just be happy. It would be so easy. I don't know why I can't. I only know there is something inside me that's fighting to come to the surface. I don't know what it is but I feel there is something vital I have to remember. It would be unfair to you if I made a commitment now. I know it seems selfish but I beg you to be patient with me. Perhaps it will go away one day and we can build a future. Can you accept that and be patient a little while longer my dear?"

Amanda leaned over and touched his face. She would have liked to slap him. Instead, she looked into his eyes and whispered, "If you ask me to wait my darling then I wait. Now if you will forgive me I think I will go to my room. It's been quite a day."

With that, she pushed her chair back and got to her feet. She gave Tim a peck on the cheek and left. As she collected her key from the reception desk, her eyes were like ice.

Back in her room she went to the mini bar and poured herself a very large gin and tonic. Throwing off her shoes she sat down at the dressing table. Raising her glass to her reflection she toasted herself and said out loud, "Soon my darling Tim I intend to make it soon. My patience has just run out."

*****

After a lonely dinner, Tim had also retired to his room. He couldn't have been more surprised when Amanda had told him they were about to become engaged before he had his accident. Then he began to think about her and all of the times she had been there for him. His parents would be very happy if he were to marry her. Maybe he should propose to her. She was a beautiful, intelligent woman. If they were married maybe the emptiness that was with him all the time would disappear. He longed to feel content. Yes, that might be the answer. Marry Amanda and start a family. If he had children he wouldn't have time to brood. That's what he would do. Tomorrow he would ask Amanda to marry him. It was about time that he started to act in a positive manner. He would also go back to work.

Starting from tomorrow he would take command of his life again.

Now he had made a decision he felt much happier. He climbed into bed and was soon asleep. Halfway through the night he woke up. There were tears running down his face. Once again the pain and emptiness was back.

He got up and went over to the window. Pulling open the curtains he stared out into the pale moonlight. He could see the sea in the distance, iron grey and still. He left the window and poured himself a glass of water. His hands shook as he lifted it to his mouth to drink.

The dream had been so vivid. He could remember every detail, he was sitting with a girl. He couldn't see her face but he could see the firelight dancing in her hair. It was the most glorious colour. He had just slipped a ring on her finger and she was looking down at her hand. His heart was so full of love he could hardly breathe. He lifted his hand to touch the silky smoothness of her hair. As his fingers reached out the scene changed and he was holding the tiller on his yacht. The waves were getting higher and he felt cold and alone. That was when he woke up.

For the rest of the night Tim paced the room. He was thrown back into a pit of despair. Why did he feel like this? Was the girl with the beautiful hair from his past or was she only a dream? If so, what made the feelings so real and so strong?

In his dream he had felt whole again. His head began to ache and he sat in a chair and put his head in his hands.

All at once he knew that this wasn't a dream. The feelings he felt were too real. This was the reason he felt only half alive. Now it made sense, now he knew why there was this emptiness in him. she was the reason. For a short while in his dream he had found the key to the reason why he had fought his way back through the fog in his brain after his accident. She was the link that had kept him going. He would find her.

All last night's resolutions were empty now. There was no way he could marry Amanda or anybody else. Not while he carried in his heart the vision of the girl with the unforgettable hair. He didn't even remember her name but he now knew that she was out there somewhere. He would find her if it took the rest of his life.

Chapter Fourteen

It had been a shock to Jenny when she learned that Tim had lost his memory. She had been very quiet when they had got back from their break.

Tina was worried that Jenny would be angry with them for not telling her about Tim earlier. She was relieved to find Jenny understood why they had kept quiet about it. In fact, Jenny seemed different, more like her old self. Bill said he thought she was over Tim at last but Tina wasn't so sure.

When Jenny had seen Tim, it had been such a shock that she had been incapable of thinking straight for a while. For days she had seen his face in her mind. He was the lucky one. He had no memory of their love while she had it forever carved on her heart.

At the end of the summer, Richard came down to spend two weeks with them.

Jenny found that she was enjoying his company more than she would have thought possible. She loved to walk with him in the evenings. The days were shorter now and the colours of autumn were stunning. They would walk the country lanes arm in arm or stroll over fields shimmering with dew. More and more Jenny was beginning to be her old self. She was at home here now. It never entered her mind to go back to the city.

Ben was doing well on his own so there was no need for Jenny to worry over him. He seemed to have grown up at last.

November came and with it the first fall of snow.

Jenny still liked to tramp the fields alone but now she didn't feel quite to lonely when she saw her solitary footsteps in the snow.

This year she didn't dread Christmas. Richard was coming down of course but not Ben. He was spending it with his new girlfriend.

It was Christmas Eve and they were all sitting round a log fire. All the presents were under the Christmas tree; Danny was tucked up in bed fast asleep. He had been in a state of high excitement all day. It was a full time job keeping him away from the presents under the tree as he was now crawling. There was a companionable silence in the room. A log shifted in the fire sending smoke up the chimney.

Richard yawned and stretched his arms above his head. "Fancy a walk Jenny?" he asked.

Jenny nodded. "Just a short one tonight. Don't forget Father Christmas will be here later. I don't want to miss him."

Richard took her hand and pulled her to the door. "Don't wait up you two," he said to Tina and Bill.

Bill grinned at Tina. "We don't intend to do we love. Don't get lost."

Out in the hall Jenny and Richard wrapped themselves up in coats and scarves. Outside it was cold but beautiful. Jenny took a deep breath and inhaled the cold air. It had stopped snowing for the moment. The moon was out and the sky was clear and filled with stars. The snow had painted everything with a coat of white. It was a magical night.

Jenny lifted her head up and gazed at the stars. "I wonder if there's another world up there," she said.

Bill smiled and tucked her hand through his arm. "Of course there is and it's Christmas Eve there too."

Jenny laughed. "I feel sorry for poor old Santa. With all that way to go I hope he has plenty of hot drinks to keep him warm.

"Don't worry," Richard replied. "Mother Christmas had given him a hot water bottle to keep him warm. Come on let's walk before we freeze to death."

With their boots making a crunching noise in the snow, they set off down the lane. They walked for a while without talking. There were trees either side of the narrow lane. The branches reached over as if making an archway. The shadows from the trees made a lacy pattern in the snow. An owl suddenly swooped down across a field. There was a small high-pitched squeal and then the owl flew up and away out of sight.

Jenny shivered and drew closer to Richard. He looked down at her and then bent and kissed her on the nose.

"Wow you're freezing," he said. "Come on let's run." Grabbing her by the hand he turned her around and together they ran all the way back home.

They took their coats and boots off and went into the kitchen. Tina and Bill had gone to bed. Keeping very quiet they made themselves hot chocolate and sat down in front of the remains of the fire. The hot drink warmed them and Jenny began to feel sleepy.

Richard put his arm around her and she laid her head on his shoulder. "It's been a lovely evening Richard but I can't keep my eyes open."

Richard stood up and pulled Jenny to her feet. "Well then it's time you went to bed." He walked with her to the door where he suddenly stopped and put his arms around her. "Let's not waste that," he said nodding towards a sprig of mistletoe that was hanging above the door. He pulled Jenny into his arms and kissed her.

Jenny closed her eyes and returned the kiss.

Richard pulled away but kept her in the circle of his arms. Looking into her eyes he said simply, "Marry me Jenny?"

She looked up at him, wanting to give him an answer but not yet able to. "Please Richard, let me give you my answer tomorrow."

He pulled her head onto his shoulder and stroked her hair. "I've waited this long I can wait a little longer."

Back in her room Jenny found she was suddenly wide awake. She pulled open the curtain and looked out of the window. She wasn't seeing the snow covered fields, she was seeing an old cedar tree with its branches sweeping onto the lawn. She saw two people sitting in its shade making plans. She leaned her head against the windowpane. Its icy coldness made her shiver. Quickly she got undressed and jumped into bed. She had left the curtain open so she sat up in bed hugging her knees and staring at the stars.

Should she marry Richard? What was the point in crying over the past? Perhaps it was time to let go. Richard had loved her for so long. She saw again in her mind the way Amanda had held onto Tim that day in Salcombe. It was as if she held a trophy. Well, perhaps Amanda had finally won. All at once she felt she couldn't go on alone anymore. She was emotionally exhausted. She needed to be loved and Richard loved her. She was tired of the feeling of such loneliness whenever Tina and Bill looked at each other in that special way. She wanted that feeling of belonging. Richard would make her feel safe again. Yes, she would marry Richard. First thing in the morning she would tell him. Pulling up the blankets she lay down to sleep. Now that she had made the decision she felt happier. There was just one thing that troubled her. Why was she crying?

Richard had never had such a wonderful Christmas. Jenny had finally agreed to be his wife. Everyone was delighted. The whole day had been perfect from beginning to end. It was a shame that Richard was due back on duty the day before New Year's Eve. Still Jenny had decided to come back with him. She wanted to tell Ben their news herself, not over the telephone.

Boxing Day had been spent making plans for the future. Richard wanted to be married by the summer. He had waited so long for Jenny, he didn't want to waste any more time. Summer seemed such a long way off so Jenny had agreed. She told herself it was what she needed. By the summer she would be Mrs Richard Evans. Richard had said he would get a job in a local hospital. They had decided to make their home in Devon. They had both grown to love it. What better place to bring up children.

Richard said he wanted to start a family as soon as possible. Little Danny had captured his heart and he longed for a son of his own.

Two days before New Year's Eve they said goodbye to Tim, Bill and little Danny and started the long drive back. The weather was bitterly cold and there was still snow on the ground. It was very late when they arrived back.

It felt strange to Jenny to be back. Ben was surprised to see them. He was even more surprised at their news. Richard stayed only long enough to drink a cup of coffee before he left for home.

Jenny sat with Ben and caught up on all the news. She noticed how he had become much more confident. He was a man now and had no need of her any more. She was pleased to notice he didn't mention Tony at all. He told her all about his new girlfriend and the new job he had. Jenny thought how good it felt not to feel responsible for Ben anymore. At last he was standing on his own two feet.

Eventually they talked themselves out and climbed the stairs to bed. When Jenny got into her old room it felt as if the months had rolled away and she had never left. Now she was wide awake. Her body was tired but her mind was active. Desperately she tossed and turned. Finally she fell asleep, only to be tortured by her dreams.

She was in Tim's arms and they were dancing round and round a beautiful tree; she was looking up into the branches and Tim was holding her tightly. Suddenly she saw someone sitting in the branches. She saw a woman launch herself out of the tree. At the same time Tim let go of her and caught the woman in his arms. The woman put her arms around Tim's neck and laughed up at him. He bent to kiss her on the lips and Jenny saw that it was Amanda he held, not her. They both turned to look at Jenny and she heard them laugh together. Jenny cried out and tried to run away but she couldn't move.

She woke up and found once again that she was crying. Once again the pain was back. She lay staring up at the ceiling. Every fibre in her body cried out for her beloved Tim. She knew now there was no more fooling herself. She could never love another man. She didn't know how she would tell Richard, she only knew she could no longer pretend she had forgotten Tim.

Richard was a good man. She had hurt him once before and now she was set to do it again. For a minute her resolve almost wavered but then she thought what her life would be if she married Richard out of pity. She did love him but only as a dear friend. He deserved to be loved the way she loved Tim.

For the first time since that fateful night she wondered what Amanda had said to Tim. Jenny had been so ashamed at what Amanda had overheard that she hadn't thought it through properly before. Maybe she should have let Amanda do her worst. Maybe she should have gone straight to Tim herself and told him everything. Had she misjudged Tim, thinking he could never forgive her? The more Jenny thought about it the more she was convinced she was right. Tim would have forgiven her. She had been a fool to listen to Amanda. The love they had shared could survive anything. She was sure of that now. Perhaps if she saw Tim again he might even regain his memory. She would never know if she didn't try. She couldn't live the rest of her life wondering.

She was more positive than she had been in months. First thing in the morning she would start to put her life back together.

It was early morning when Jenny hired a car and set out on the road to Tim's parent's house. The weather was still freezing but Jenny didn't feel the cold. There was a warmth in her heart that hadn't been there for a while. Tomorrow was New Year's Eve what a perfect time to start again.

Jenny looked at her watch and thought it may be a little early to call. She decided to stop and have breakfast. Suitably refreshed, she resumed her journey. The miles flew by and Jenny was lost in dreams of the future. She couldn't wait to see her darling Tim again. Now she was strong enough to face up to anyone who opposed her. A smile was on her lips as she drove on.

There was black ice on the road and Jenny had no way of seeing it as she drove the car around the bend. She tried to gain control as the car skidded towards the other side of the road.

A man walking his dog in the field heard the impact as the car hit the tree. He ran over but one glance was enough to tell him there was nothing he could do. The man gently laid her on the grass and covered her with a blanket that was on the back seat of the car. He took out of his pocket a mobile phone and called the police and an ambulance. He stood waiting beside the body.

The sound of horses hooves made him look up. A man and a woman were approaching. They reined in their horses and approached in single file along the grass verge. The woman was in front. He saw her eyes widen as she looked at the still form on the frost covered grass. He saw the man's face turn pale as he looked down at the red-gold tresses spilling out from under the blanket.

Amanda knew immediately who it was. She felt no pity. Looking over at Tim she knew she had to get him away fast. He seemed mesmerised. Amanda reached over and took the reins from Tim's hand and led his horse away.

She didn't look back but she knew the accident had only just happened...

Chapter Fifteen

Ben looked at the lovely girl sitting opposite him at the breakfast table and once again was transported back into the past. At times he could hardly believe that this was his daughter. She was so like his sister Jenny. It was as if his beloved sister had been reincarnated to ease his pain. His mind once again went back over the years to that dreadful time when Jenny had died. He had been very young then, younger than Laura was now. For a while he had gone completely off the rails. It was Richard that had helped him pull himself together again. Ben would always remember how Richard had taken charge of everything, in spite of being heartbroken he had taken Ben under his wing. He had been there when Ben had run riot with his so-called friends. He had been there to pick up the pieces when Ben had almost had a breakdown. It was Richard who had sat up with him night after night while he had raged at the whole world for taking Jenny. Only later had Ben realised just how much Richard was going through as well.

Eventually Ben had picked himself up and thanks to Richard had emerged into a grown man.

Two months after Jenny died, Ben's new girlfriend Eve told him she was pregnant so they decided to get married. It didn't work out and when the baby was just over a year old Ben had arrived home one day to find baby Laura alone in the house crying in her cot. He also found a note informing him that his wife had run off with the man who used to work in the local pub. Ben wasn't that much bothered by it all really as he knew that his marriage had been a mistake. The only good thing to come out of it was his daughter. Ben was totally besotted with little Laura and he was determined that she should want for nothing. He found a woman that was more than willing to look after Laura; she had just lost her husband and was very glad to earn some money.

Laura was a happy child and she thrived on the love and attention that was showered on her.

Ben worked hard and eventually he was able to buy a plot of

derelict land and with the help of his friendly bank manager, built two houses and sold them at a good profit. He had repeated this process a few times, each time building bigger and better houses until he had made a fortune. He had also built himself a good reputation for quality work and was now a well liked and trusted man in the community. He had done all this on his own. He had fulfilled the promise he had made to himself for Laura. She had never wanted for anything. She was now a very talented artist and was fast building a name for herself. Her work was becoming more and more in demand. Ben was still only in his early forties and there were a few women that had set their cap at him but Ben thought only of his daughter. For him it was a case of once bitten twice shy. He had never bothered to try to find his wife; he had no idea if she was alive or dead. He had stopped thinking of her years ago.

His thoughts went back to Richard.

Richard had gone on to be a surgeon and five years ago had taken a position in a hospital in Capetown, South Africa, there he had met and married a local girl.

Ben was delighted when Richard had written and asked him to be his best man, and he and Laura had flown out to attend the wedding and then had the holiday of a lifetime. Ben liked Richard's new wife but he knew Richard would always have a special place in his heart that would forever belong to Jenny.

Ben was jolted back from his memories as Laura pushed her chair back from the breakfast table and rushed over to give him a quick kiss on the cheek.

"Bye Dad," she said. "See you later."

"Are you off already?" Ben asked.

Laura put her hand on his shoulder. "I did tell you last night Daddy, I have an appointment at ten, see you at dinner." She kissed the top of his head and was out of the door in a flash.

Ben sighed and poured himself another cup of coffee. The house always seemed empty when Laura was out. When she was in she spent most of her time in her studio at the top of the house. Ben was really very proud of his lovely daughter. Sometimes he was allowed to watch Laura paint. These were the best times for Ben. He was always amazed at Laura's talent. She would lose herself for hours while she worked.

Her paintings would spring to life. If she were paining a portrait,

Ben could almost see it breathe. If she did a painting of the sea he could almost feel the wind as it beat the waves away from the sand.

He knew Laura would rather be alone to paint so he tried not to wander up to her studio in the evenings. But sometimes he would take her a cup of tea and a sandwich just so that he could get to sit and watch. This ruse didn't always work. Once Laura had given him a canvas and some brushes and told him to have a go himself.

Ben had tried but ended up with more paint on him than on the canvas. Moreover, when he showed Laura his painting of a sheep, she thought it was a table. They had almost had hysterics that evening. After that Ben had decided to forego a career in art and stick to what he did best. They both agreed he would be no great loss to the art world.

*****

Amanda sat in front of her dressing table and scrutinised her reflection. She lifted her head to the right, then turned to the left, inspecting closely. She was on the whole quite pleased with what she saw. She was still a beautiful woman. Nobody could say she didn't still take care of herself.

The years had been good to her. She had married the man she had always loved. In fact she was still in love with him after all these years. They had a son that she doted on and despite her spoiling had grown into a charming young man.

Amanda had never wanted more children. Her husband would have liked at least one more but unbeknown to him, Amanda had made quite sure there would be no other children. The truth was she hadn't wanted to share her husband with children. She had only become pregnant because she thought it would bind her husband more closely to her. Once the baby had been born, Amanda had been surprised at the intensity of her love for him.

As he grew older Amanda grew more possessive. At times, it had been the cause of many an argument between mother and son. Amanda never seemed to like any of her son's girlfriends. If they were brought home to meet her, Amanda was always pleasant to them in front of her son but none of them lasted very long.

She had always wanted to be mistress of his house and she loved ruling over her husband and son. The last thing she wanted was another woman in the house.

Her mind went back to the woman that had nearly wrecked her happiness. She still hated Jenny Woods, even though she had been dead for years. Amanda could never forget how much Tim loved that little shop girl. She knew that he would never love her in the same way. She had done so much to win him but deep down she knew she was second best.

She closed her eyes and her mind was back in the past again. She could see Jenny and Tim in each other's arms as they danced, they were oblivious of everyone as they looked into each other's eyes. As they danced, the new ring on Jenny's finger would catch the light and burst its brilliance over them. Tim held her as if she were the most precious porcelain. Every now and then he would bend his head and kiss her gently and she would look up at him, her face glowing with love.

Amanda had thought she had forgotten that night but it had come flooding back to her. Never had she hated that little shop girl more than on that night. It had been the hardest thing she had ever done to wish them both well. She had always loved Tim. Another image flashed into her mind. Vibrant hair spilling over the frosty grass on a winter's morning. This had been the beginning of hope for Amanda. Now Jenny was dead there was no fear what Tim would do if he recovered his memory.

Amanda, now more than ever, made sure she was always by his side. She protected him, entertained him, and shielded him from the press when they discovered Jenny had died. She made herself responsible for anything and everything in his life. Both of their parents were only too pleased by the way things were going between them.

Finally, Tim had succumbed to Amanda and they had been married.

For years Amanda had worried about Tim, but as time went by she finally had let the past slide into oblivion, or almost.

Amanda stood up and walked to her wardrobe. She must stop thinking of the past. She selected one of her favourite dresses, tossed it onto the bed and went into the bathroom to take a shower. As she slipped out of her robe she looked at herself in the mirror and smiled. She still had a good body, she still had her beloved Tim, why should she let the spectre of Jenny Woods bother her now, after all, she had won hadn't she? Turning on the tap she stepped into the shower.

*****

Tim stood at the window looking at the magnificent cedar tree.
He loved that old tree. It seemed to have a power over him; he was
always drawn to it, especially when he felt troubled. Just sitting under
its enormous branches was enough to soothe him and gave him a
feeling of calm. It was an old friend; one that would always be there
for him and would never let him down. Tim had seen photos of
himself as a small boy sitting in its branches. It was strange to look at
a part of his past and not remember it.

Over the years he can come to accept most of it. Everyone
thought he had come to terms with remembering only half of his life
but in his heart, Tim knew he could never be at peace with himself.

At times he would feel guilty. He would think of the way
Amanda had stood by him. It must have been hell for her when he
couldn't remember who she was. She had been so patient with him,
Tim had thought he must have been very much in love with her before
his accident. There had seemed no other choice for him but to marry
Amanda out of gratitude. Nobody had ever guessed that Tim was
unhappy. His parents had died about five years ago within months of
each other, they had always believed that Tim and Amanda were the
perfect pair. They had everything. They had moved into Tim's family
home after his parents had died and the house had remained exactly as
it had always been.

As he stood there lost in thought he saw his son come into view.
He watched as Adam threw himself on the grass under the tree and
open a book. All at once Tim had the strangest feeling. It was as if he
were locked in that old dream again. He had almost a feeling of panic.
He felt as if he was poised on the edge of the world and he wanted to
leap into space. There was still the shadowy figure of a woman on the
edge of the dream; she had never gone away.

Abruptly he turned from the window and went to find what was
keeping Amanda. They were going to be late if she didn't hurry. They
were having dinner with Amanda's parents. Tim always enjoyed
seeing Elizabeth and George.

They were now in their eighties but were still good company.

Amanda was halfway down the stairs; as usual she was looking elegant in a tight fitting evening gown of black lace. It clung to her body, showing off her still slender figure. The neck was scooped very low and the sleeves were full length. Round her neck she wore a stunning diamond necklace.

Tim gave a low whistle when he saw her. Amanda gave him a little curtsey.

"So I was worth waiting for then."

"As ever my dear," he replied. "Now we really must hurry or we will be late."

Amanda walked over to a crystal bowl full of pale yellow roses. She selected one and walked over to Tim. Reaching up she put it in his buttonhole. "That's your reward for being so patient. Now you look even more handsome."

Tim looked down at his wife and felt a surge of guilt. He wished he could shake off the feeling that he was always acting a part. He made up his mind that he would try his best to forget everything for now and just enjoy the evening ahead.

He bent his head and lifted his lapel to smell the delicate perfume of the rose, then offering his arm to Amanda, escorted her out to the car.

*****

Adam opened his eyes. He realised he had fallen asleep. He looked at his watch then leaped up. He would just be in time if he hurried. He ran into the house and up to his room. Within half an hour he was striding along the path by the river and there she was. His face lit up at the sight of her. She saw him walking towards her and she stood up and ran to meet him. He took her in his arms and they kissed. Adam held her tightly, then held her at arms length and smiled down at her.

"I have been waiting for that all day," he told her.

She laughed up into his face. "So how come you are late then Mr Knight?"

He gently pulled her onto the bench. "Because Miss Woods I fell asleep and I didn't want to wake up because I was dreaming of you."

Laura held his hand. "In that case I forgive you. Now let me tell you my news. I have just sold my latest painting and the buyer wants another two painting besides. It means I won't have much spare time for the next few weeks so you will have to let me get on. That means no distractions. I won't be able to see you much darling. I promise I will ring though."

Adam's face fell. "I'm glad for you darling but I must confess it will be hell not seeing you. I don't know how I shall survive without you."

Laura gave him a hug. "Absence makes the heart fonder they say."

Adam looked into her eyes and Laura could see he wasn't joking as he bent his head and leaned his forehead on hers. "My darling girl, don't you know how every minute apart from you is an eternity? Do your painting and when you are finished we will celebrate in a very special way."

Laura closed her eyes and kissed him. She too would find it hard to be apart from Adam. She knew she loved him with all her heart but she at least would be able to lose herself in her work so the time would pass quickly.

They had only known each other a few months but it seemed as if they had met a lifetime ago.

They had met at an art exhibition and as they had discovered later, it had been a case of love at first sight for both of them. Although they had been seeing each other, Laura had not met Adam's parents yet. Laura had taken Adam home to meet her father and had been surprised and a little hurt at the reaction from him. She had put it down to jealousy in the end. After, all her father had brought her up single-handed and now there was another man in her life. It was perhaps only natural.

She was convinced that her father would come round. It did, however, make her wonder how Adam's parents would react to her. That was one of the reasons Laura had put off meeting Mr and Mrs Knight, but she knew she would have to meet them soon.

She suddenly sprang up and pulled Adam to his feet. "Come on then, let's make the most of this evening, I'm starving, let's go and eat."

Adam as usual was only too happy to go along with Laura. He suddenly realised that he was also starving.

Chapter Sixteen

Ben looked up from his book as Laura walked into the room. He caught his breath as he looked at her. She was so like Jenny it made his heart miss a beat.

Laura was wearing a jade evening dress; her short hair was vibrantly alive with the same colour as his sister's. It framed her small face and made her green eyes look ever bigger. Just like Jenny had been, she was unaware how beautiful she was.

Ben stood up and walked over to her. "Oh Laura you look lovely," he said.

"Thank you Daddy," she said. "I feel so nervous at the thought of meeting Adam's parents, I need a boost to my confidence. I must say it feels good to dress up again after spending weeks covered in paint."

"Before you go," Ben said, "there is something I want to tell you. I should have told you before but I never got round to it. Come and sit down."

Laura looked at her watch. "You will have to be quick Daddy. Adam will be here shortly."

Ben cleared his throat. "I think you should know that your Aunt Jenny knew Adam's parents."

Laura looked up at Ben. "I know that Daddy, she used to work at the store, you told me that years ago."

Ben walked over to the window and gazed out. "I mean she knew them socially. She spent a lot of time with them. That was when Adam's grandparents were alive. She used to stay at the house quite a lot."

Laura frowned. "I don't understand. How did she get to know Adam's family?"

Ben ran his fingers through his hair. He was just about to speak when the doorbell rang. Laura jumped up.

"That will be Adam. You will have to tell me the rest some other time Daddy we can't possibly be late tonight. She gave him a quick peck on the cheek and was out of the door before Ben could say a word.

Ben poured himself a drink and sat down. He had been worrying about what to tell Laura. He knew he would have to tell her something because Adam's parents would know who Laura was as soon as they saw her. He was reluctant to bring up the past. It still hurt when he thought how Jenny had suffered when Tim had had his accident. Ben was sure that there was a lot he didn't know. He knew Adam's mother had hated Jenny because she had wanted Tim for herself. Jenny had told him that much. Should he tell Laura? After a long time spent in thought, he decided to leave the past alone. He hoped Amanda Knight would think the same. He hoped the years had softened Amanda and that she would not let the past prejudice her against Laura. After all, surely all a mother would want is for her son to be happy and who could not love a sweet girl like Laura? Just seeing them together could gladden the heart. With a sigh, Ben got up to pour himself another drink.

Little did he know about the heart of Amanda Knight, it was as well that he was unaware of the cunning and twisted mind she had and lengths to which she would go to keep what she thought was hers.

He wouldn't have been able to enjoy his quiet evening at home if he had been able to see into the future. Had this been possible, he would have seen that Amanda Knight was capable of making his beloved daughter as heartbroken as she had made his sister.

*****

It had been a shock for Amanda when Adam had told her about his girlfriend. At first she had thought she must be mistaken and that Laura Woods was no relation to that awful shop girl. Then after questioning Adam she realised there was no mistake. After all these years she was about to be confronted with the past. What made it even worse was that it was her own son that had unwittingly been the cause of her nightmares once again. What should she do about it?

In the end Amanda had decided to leave things alone for a while.

She looked at her husband as he handed her a drink and thought how handsome he looked still. He came and sat opposite her, stretching out his legs and crossing his ankles.

"So we finally get to meet Adam's girlfriend. This one is something special so he says. We must make her feel welcome."

Amanda raised her eyebrows. "Are you trying to tell me I don't know how to entertain a guest in my own house? After all, that's all she is, just another guest."

Tim sat up straight. "Darling I meant no such thing. You are always the perfect hostess, as you well know. As I said before this particular girl seems to mean a lot to Adam judging by the way he speaks."

Amanda was saved from answering by the arrival of their son with the girl she didn't at all want to meet. Amanda and Tim stood up. Laura stood before her and Amanda gasped. She felt sick. She was the image of that creature. For the first time in her life Amanda didn't feel in control. She felt the blood rush from her face and her legs turn weak. She was aware of Tim's arm around her as he gently lowered her back into the chair. She closed her eyes. What if Tim looked at Laura and remembered? Was it all over? She felt powerless. She made a great effort and recovered herself. Putting her hand to her forehead she gave Tim a smile.

"Sorry darling, I must have got up too quickly. I'm fine now." Turning to Laura, she held out her hand but did not get up from her chair. "What must you think of me my dear? I can assure you that doesn't usually happen."

When Laura shook her hand, Amanda wanted to scream at her to get our of her house. Instead she smiled up at her.

Now Laura was smiling at Timm and Amanda felt as if her heart was going to stop beating. She held her breath and watched as Tim kissed Laura on the cheek. She didn't hear what they were saying to each other. She was aware of her heart pounding and she thought they could almost hear it. She watched Tim closely but there was no recognition in his eyes. She let our her breath and closed her eyes in relief.

The whole evening seemed unreal to Amanda. They all sat round the table and ate dinner together. Adam hardly took his eyes off Laura. They had that special look of two people in love. Amanda realised this girl would take more getting rid of than Adam's other girlfriends. However, she would have to go.

Laura, however, was feeling much more relaxed. She liked Adam's father immediately. His mother seemed very nice but her smile didn't reach her eyes when she smiled. Dinner was not the ordeal Laura was expecting and despite earlier misgivings, she ate heartily. The food was wonderful and Laura had more than her usual one glass of wine. Adam's father was charming. He insisted on opening one of his favourite vintage wines in honour of the occasion. Laura felt so relaxed with him, and when he asked her to call them Amanda and Tim, Laura found it very easy to do so.

After dinner, Adam gave her a tour of the house. Laura thought it was beautiful. Then they wandered around the garden. The evening was cool and sweet with the scent of flowers. Under the big cedar tree they stopped and Adam pulled Laura gently into his arms and kissed her. After, he held her close and they were content to just savour the moment.

Looking up into the branches of the tree, Adam said, "I believe there is something magical about this old tree. It's been here forever. My father loves it. If he is ever feeling down he seems to gravitate towards it."

Laura looked up and through its branches she could see the moon. It looked as if it were suspended at the very top of the tree.

"I can feel the magic Adam," she said. "I want to climb up and reach for the moon to give you as a memento of this evening."

Adam held her tighter. "Darling, I need nothing to remind me of tonight. It will be the first of many memories to store for when we are old and grey and our children have flown the nest."

Laura couldn't answer because there was such a feeling of happiness inside her she thought that she would burst.

At the end of the evening, when Adam drove her home, he held her close and told her again how much he loved her.

Later, before she drifted off to sleep, Laura wondered why she had ever been worried about meeting the Knights. After all, they were all charming.

Chapter Seventeen

Amanda was not in a good mood the next day. She had tossed and turned all night. She was still shaken up at the resemblance of Laura to her Aunt. She was so sure that Tim might have noticed something. She had been terrified that it could start some stirrings in Tim's memory. The relief of it was unbelievable.

Something would have to be done about the situation and quickly. She didn't intend to spend the rest of her life feeling as if she were walking on eggshells.

Adam came down late for breakfast. Amanda and Tim were almost finished when he came in.

He kissed Amanda good morning and sat and helped himself to coffee. He looked at his parents over the rim of his cup. Tim put down the letter he was reading.

"Well you look pleased with yourself today Adam."

Adam put his cup down and resting his elbows on the table put his hands under his chin. "What did you two think of Laura?" he asked.

Tim answered at once. "I thought she was a charming girl Adam and a bit of a stunner."

Adam beamed at him then turned to Amanda. "What about you Mother?" he asked.

Amanda wiped her mouth with her napkin playing for time. "She seems very nice dear. Now if you will excuse me I have things to do."

She was just about to leave when Adam pushed his chair away and stood up.

"While I have you both together I want to tell you that I intend to ask Laura to marry me."

Tim stood up and going to his son shook him warmly by the hand. "Good for you Adam," he said. "You make a fine couple. I wish you both well." Turning to Amanda he said, "Well darling, what do you think of that? Our son is to be a married man."

Amanda gave him a cool look and ignoring the remark turned to her son. "I want you to be happy Adam," she said. "Marriage is a big step. Just give yourself time before you rush into anything. You are both so young, what's the rush?"

Adam just grinned at her. "If I wait ten or twenty years I will still want to marry Laura so why waste time? Anyway, I intend to ask her very soon."

Amanda put her hand on his shoulder and gave him a kiss on the cheek. "Well at least have some breakfast darling. That won't make any difference to the next twenty years." Lifting up her chin she walked regally out of the room.

Amanda waited until Tim and Adam had left the house then she picked up the phone. Directory inquiries soon gave her the number. After the third ring Laura answered. She was surprised to discover it was Amanda. She was pleased when Amanda invited her round for morning coffee.

"Just the two of us without the men."

Laura arrived on time and Amanda opened the door to her as if she had been waiting behind it for Laura to arrive.

"I thought we would have coffee on the terrace," Amanda said, leading the way.

Laura followed, feeling a little in awe of her hostess.

They seated themselves down and Amanda poured the coffee. She looked Laura straight in the eye and there was no warmth in the smile she gave her. Laura started to feel uncomfortable.

"It would appear that my son thinks he is in love with you my dear," she said.

Laura felt the colour flood her face and for the life of her she could find nothing to say.

Amanda went on, "I can't blame him for that as you are quite an attractive young woman However, there can be no question of an alliance with you."

Laura gasped in amazement. Before she could speak Amanda leaned over and touched her arm and in a kinder voice continued. "Don't think it has anything to do with me not liking you my dear. I think you are charming and if things were different I would be only too pleased to let things progress. However, when you hear what I have to tell you, you will understand." Leaning back in her chair she gazed into space as if she were looking back down the years. She took out a tiny lace handkerchief and dabbed her eyes.

Laura sat totally bemused waiting to hear what on earth she was going to say.

Amanda gave a sigh and looked at Laura. "I must tell you something that is very painful for me to speak of. Please don't speak until I have finished. The truth is I knew your Aunt. I first met her when she was working at our department store. Of course I wasn't married then but my family were the Knights oldest friends. Tim and I were inseparable most of our lives. We fell in love when we were very young indeed. It was taken for granted that we would marry. Your Aunt and I became friends in spite of it being frowned on by Tim's father. I used to invite her to parties or maybe to dinner. I thought nothing of it, she was my friend. At least I thought she was."

Amanda put her hands over her eyes and leaned her elbows on the table.

Laura sat straight up in her chair, wondering what on earth this was all about.

Amanda carried on, "I was the one that introduced your Aunt to my husband. As soon as she set eyes on him I could tell she was besotted with him. Of course he didn't notice at first, then when she started calling him on the phone constantly and trying to be alone with him it became obvious. At first I thought she would grow out of her infatuation with him. Later I realised how serious it was. She was quite a pretty girl and I don't mean to be unkind my dear but she knew how to use her looks. Tim was very young and I suppose that's why he succumbed."

Amanda suddenly stood up and went over to Laura and put her hand on her shoulder. "I wish there was an easy way to tell you this my dear but there isn't. Your Aunt finally seduced Tim. Of course he was full of remorse after and came to me to make a clean breast of it and to beg my forgiveness. We got engaged soon after that. A few months after that your Aunt came to me and told me she was pregnant."

Laura was stunned.

Amanda walked round and took Laura's hands. "My dear you must prepare yourself for a shock. When Jenny told me her news, she asked if I would be able to get Tim or his father to give her money. She said she had left it too late to have an abortion."

Laura was too amazed to realise that it was the first time Amanda had used Jenny's name. She looked into the eyes of Amanda trying to read her feelings but they were inscrutable. Even now Amanda hated to speak that dreaded name.

She continued with her lies. "Of course I gave her as much money as I could as well as Tim. This made her quite wealthy from her point of view, anyway she had the baby but she didn't want to stay around any more. Maybe it was all that money. I don't know. One day, a few weeks after she had given birth, she just went. She left the baby with her brother. That baby was you my dear. Ben took you on as if you were his own. He didn't want anyone to find out about his sister so he married to give you a stable upbringing. I'm sorry to tell you but you must see that you can't see Adam again. He is your half brother."

Laura felt as if she had been turned to ice. She didn't hear anything more. She sat and stared at this woman in front of her. How could she sit there looking so elegant? Looking as if she were discussing what new hat to buy, not telling her this horrendous story. Laura was looking at that cold face in front of her. She suddenly saw there was no compassion in it. The eyes that looked into hers looked as cold as the ice that had crept into Laura's heart.

She shook her head from side to side and covered her ears with her hands, trying to stop the words that were pouring out of that cruel mouth that was just inches from her. She wanted to scream at her to stop. She wanted Adam to be here, to hold her and tell her it wasn't true. She wanted to run to her father and have him tell her this was all lies. Instead, she just sat as if turned to stone. She had no idea how long she had been sitting there. She became aware that Amanda was talking to her but she couldn't take anything in. At last she stood up and without a word to Amanda, walked away.

She couldn't remember how she got home. All she could see was Amanda's face with her cold eyes staring into hers and her voice going on and on saying those awful things that had torn her world apart.

Chapter Eighteen

Richard emerged from the swimming pool and threw himself down onto the grass beside Laura. He saw she had fallen asleep so he took the opportunity to study her face. He was glad that the tense, drawn look she had when she had arrived had faded. Now she had a healthy tan and she looked as if she had been getting to sleep at night.

The years had been good to Richard. He had never been more handsome, he still had a full head of hair even though it was threaded with silver. The lines around his warm brown eyes only seemed to enhance his rugged looks. He had looked after himself and so had maintained his physique. In fact, he was the type of man that grew more attractive with age.

He had been surprised and delighted when Laura had phoned six weeks ago to ask if she could visit. When he had met Laura at the airport, he had known at once there was something very wrong. he didn't ask what, he knew she would tell him in her own time.

Richard had spoken to Ben on the phone and it was clear that even he had no idea what had changed his daughter so drastically in so short a time. They had both decided to give Laura as much time as she needed. When she was ready, she would confide in them, meanwhile Richard and his wife Jane were only too happy to look after her.

As he looked at her he was suddenly transported back over the years to the time he had spent in Devon with Jenny and for a moment he once again felt the unspeakable heartbreak he thought had passed.

Laura was so much like her. Richard closed his eyes and gave himself up to the past. He still loved her, he knew he always would. He had a whole new life now and he was more than satisfied with his work. He had met Jane at work. They had become friends and after a while they started dating. Richard had grown used to Jane being around so it seemed natural that he should propose. Jane was head over heels in love with him so they were married. They had a beautiful home and were happy together.

Jane still worked at the hospital. The only cloud on the horizon was Jane being unable to have children. This had been a bitter disappointment to Jane and ironic as she was a gynaecologist, but in time they had both come to accept it. Richard loved Jane but it was not the same love that he had felt for Jenny, that was a once in a lifetime love. Jane was so different from Jenny, she was confident, outgoing and knew exactly what she wanted from life. Richard was very content with the way his life was going now.

He was brought back to the present when he felt a hand on his arm. Laura was awake. She smiled at him and pointed. Jane was walking towards them carrying a tray with drinks on. Richard jumped up and took the tray from her.

"What did I do to deserve you," he asked as he kissed her on the cheek.

Jane laughed. "Just lucky I guess." She sat down and Richard handed out the drinks. He held up his glass.

"To us," he said.

Laura and Jane held up their glasses and as one echoed "to us."

The garden was so beautiful; it filled the senses and left each one with a feeling of deep tranquillity and serenity. Each one of them succumbed to the magic of the day.

In the evening they enjoyed a superb dinner and ended up sitting under the stars for a last nightcap. Laura felt more rested and relaxed than she had in weeks. That night she slept soundly until the sunshine intruded into her room to wake her.

Laura went downstairs the next morning feeling hungrier than she had for ages. She had the place to herself as Jane and Richard had left for work. She went into the kitchen and made herself a hearty breakfast. Today she felt full of energy and all of a sudden she had the urge to paint. She ran upstairs to get a hat and soon she was in the car Jane had loaned her and was heading for Capetown to buy some artist materials.

An hour later, with her purchases in the boot, she was driving along the road with Table Mountain on her left and the most stunning views to her right. She eventually parked, got out of the car and stood drinking in the wild beauty before her. She was standing against a wooden fence. Way down below, the turquoise sea crashed, foaming white breakers against rocks that looked as if they had been there forever.

Laura stood spellbound. If she hadn't been an artist she would still have marvelled at the colours of the rocks, the wildflowers, the sweep of grass and the sand that looked as if it had been poured there among the rocks by a giant hand as an afterthought.

The painting that Laura did that day was special. In years to come she was to have many offers from people who wanted to buy it but she could not bring herself to part with it. She felt she had put part of herself into it. There was something magical about it. She didn't realise the irony in being so affected by the sea. She had no way of knowing it was the beautiful but unpredictable sea that had taken away from her Aunt Jenny any chance of happiness when it had taken away the memory of the only man she could truly love. It had changed the life of lots of people in a split second, including her own.

Laura arrived back just in time to have a quick shower before dinner.

Richard and Jane were delighted to discover that she had started painting again. They both felt Laura was on the way back to her old self again. They were both so wrong.

Chapter Nineteen

Over the next few weeks. Laura regained her appetite and was sleeping well. She had also started to put on weight. At first she thought it was because she was feeling more relaxed, then out of the blue realisation hit her. She had been dressing for dinner and was very cross when she found her favourite dress was too tight. It had been a while since she had worn it and now it wouldn't do up. She scanned her body in the mirror and the blood drained from her face. She was pregnant. She had ignored all the signs, too distraught to notice what was going on with her body. Now she could no longer ignore it. Her mind was in turmoil. What was she going to do? How could she have this baby if the father was her own half brother? She was overcome with a feeling of nausea and running to the bathroom was violently sick.

Laura stared at her face in the mirror. How was she to live with this? She still wasn't over the fact that Adam was her half brother, what would happen now?

Feeling as if her whole world had come to an end, Laura sat on the window seat and with unseeing eyes, stared out at the garden below.

Laura didn't hear the knock at the door. Jane had come up to see what was keeping Laura so long. She opened the door and poked her head around it.

"Just wondered where you were," she said. "Dinner is ready."

Laura didn't seem to hear so Jane walked over and touched Laura on the shoulder.

"Penny for your thoughts, you seem miles away."

Laura spun round and to her surprise as much as Jane's. burst into tears. At first Jane let her cry, thinking it was the aftermath of Laura's problem. When Laura showed no sign of stopping, Jane started to worry. She gently guided Laura over to the bed and sat beside her. She put her arms around her and stroking the hair away from her forehead rocked her as if she were a little girl.

Gradually Laura stopped crying. Jane went into the bathroom and came back with a face cloth. Laura wiped her face and stood up. Walking over to the dressing table, she picked up a brush and without thinking, started to brush her hair.

Jane came over and put her hands on Laura's shoulders. "Do you want to tell me what this is all about sweetheart?" she said.

Laura reached up and took Jane's hand. Her eyes brimmed with tears again as she looked into the mirror at their reflections.

Jane saw such misery in Laura's face, her heart went out to her. "What can I do to help? Do you feel ill; would you like to talk to Richard? Tell me what I can do for you?"

The look of love and concern on Jane's face was just too much for Laura. She spun out of the chair and threw herself on her knees. Throwing her arms around Jane's waist she once again burst into tears.

Now Jane was really getting worried. She knelt down and cradled Laura in her arms. Finally Laura spoke. Her voice barely above a whisper, "Jane I think I'm pregnant and I don't know what to do."

Very gently Jane took Laura's hands and pulled her into a chair. She cupped her hands around Laura's face and looked into her eyes. "The first thing to do is make an appointment for you to see me at the hospital. Let's find out for sure if you are pregnant. Remember you have changed your whole way of life lately so you may be worrying over nothing."

Laura gave a weak smile. "I could be wrong of course but I have a feeling I'm not."

"Now," said Jane standing up, "do you feel like washing your face and coming down to dinner? Richard must be ravenous by now. Try not to worry anymore and remember we are always here for you." Bending down she kissed Laura on the cheek and then left the room.

Laura was glad she had confided in Jane. It was good to know she wasn't quite as alone now. All of a sudden she felt hungry. Perhaps it was all the crying; anyway she was ready for dinner. Five minutes later she was on her way downstairs.

The next morning she was up early enough to have breakfast with Jane and Richard before they went to work. Before she left Jane told Laura she was under orders not to worry.

Halfway through the morning Laura had a phone call from Jane. She had booked an appointment for her late in the afternoon.

Now she was sitting in the waiting room, which was now empty, pretending to read a magazine.

A door opened and Laura looked up in time to see Jane poke her head round. She smiled at Laura and opened the door wide. Laura stood up and walked into her consulting room.

An hour later both women were having coffee in Jane's office. Laura couldn't cry anymore. What good would tears do anyway?

*****

Jane lay on her back in bed staring into the darkness. She had given up trying to sleep. Richard had fallen asleep as soon as his head touched the pillow. She envied him his ability to sleep; she had not had a good night for weeks. In a few weeks Laura's baby would be born. At times she didn't know how she could bear it. She longed to have Richard's child. They both wanted a baby so much. She was very fond of Laura and was happy to share her home with her for a while but Laura was looking for a place of her own now. It had been decided that Laura would stay with Jane and Richard for a while after the baby was born. Then when she had regained her strength, move into her own home.

When Laura had first discovered she was pregnant, Jane had been tempted to beg Laura to let her and Richard adopt the baby but Richard had been totally against the idea. They had never asked who the father was and Laura had never spoken about him. There was still too much pain in her eyes, also Jane knew she cried a lot at night still.

Slipping out of bed, Jane slipped into a pale blue silk robe and made her way down to the kitchen. She made herself a cup of tea and carried it into the sitting room. Drawing back the curtain she stood gazing at the garden bathed in moonlight.

It was a beautiful night. The day had been really hot but now the moon had poured its silver light over her domain, making things deliciously cool. Jane couldn't resist the silent splendour. Wandering out, she stood still and inhaled deeply. The scent of the flowers wafted over her. The grass felt wonderful beneath her bare feet. She made her way to her favourite spot in the garden and sat on a bench.

It was a magical night. She could feel the tension leave her and lifting up her face to the velvet night, sat in wonder at the millions of stars above her. For a while she was at one with the night. A Moon

Goddess who ruled the world for tonight. She was surrounded with harmony and beauty. As the night finally began to give up her reign to the pale dawn, Jane went back inside. The time she had spent alone in the garden had filled her with such peace she felt renewed and strong enough to face the future with the problems it would bring. After all, she had Richard by her side whatever happened. Poor Laura may be about to give birth but where was her true love.

Counting her blessings, Jane went back upstairs and slipped quietly into bed. Minutes late she was fast asleep.

*****

Laura, however, was still tossing and turning. She was unable to get comfortable. She felt as if she had been pregnant for years. Whenever she thought about the baby she became filled with panic, wondering if he or she would have any abnormalities. It was too painful still to think about Adam and so she would try to push him out of her mind. She had never told Richard or Jane who the father was. She had made up her mind over the past few months that she would keep this baby no matter what. She was able to earn good money through her painting and she was determined to make a new life for them both in a new country. She still hadn't told her father about the baby.

She had written lots of letters trying to tell him but had torn them up. Now Laura had decided that she would go back home when the baby was born to explain, then return to her new life. She was hoping her father might return with her and his new grandchild.

Laura missed her father so much. She would dream about him and the next day would feel so guilty. She felt she had let him down. Laura would weep for the times they had together. They were so happy just the two of them. She could never imagine Tim Knight as her father. She would never stop thinking of Ben as anyone other than her own father. Still, Laura couldn't help wondering how he would feel when he knew the truth about her birth was out. Would he still want anything to do with her when he knew about the baby. Would she still be his girl?

Chapter Twenty

Adam was driving much too fast. He was on his way to see Laura's father. He was very worried. There had been no word from Laura for three days. She hadn't even telephoned him. Normally she would say if she had a painting to finish and didn't want to be disturbed, but he wasn't aware she was working on one at the moment. He stopped his car near her house and walked up to the front door. Her father opened the door and seemed surprised to see him.

"Come in lad," he said.

Adam followed him into the sitting room and sat in the chair Ben indicated.

"I'm here to see Laura," Adam said.

Ben looked puzzled, "Don't you know she's not here. I was going to come to see you myself to see if you could put me in the picture as to what's going on."

Now it was Adam's turn to look puzzled. "I don't understand you," he said feeling even more worried than when he arrived. "Where is she?"

Ben turned and started pacing the floor. For the first time Adam noticed how miserable Ben looked. He ran his hands through his hair and turned to Adam. "All I know is she came in here three days ago, packed her bags and told me she was going to South Africa to stay with her Uncle Richard and his wife for a while. You could have knocked me down with a feather I can tell you. It's not like my Laura to do that. Something's wrong I know but she wouldn't say what. I could see she was very upset, try as she would hide it. It broke my heart to see her go like that. If you're behind it young man I need to know now."

Adam was stunned. This didn't make any sense at all. He went over in his mind all the things they had said the last time they had been together. He could remember nothing that would have upset Laura. He looked up at Ben. "I have no idea what's wrong. The last time we were together, everything was fine. In fact more than fine, we were about to announce our engagement."

Ben stopped his pacing and flopped into a chair. "That only makes things more of a puzzle." He leaned his head back and closed his eyes.

Adam noticed that he looked very tired and much older. He stood up and walking over to the sideboard poured Ben a large scotch. He took it and looking up at Adam said in a voice that shook with worry, "What would make her do this, why would she run off? I'm at my wits end Adam. I can't think straight anymore. I'm so tired." He tipped his glass up and swallowed his drink in one go.

Adam took his empty glass and put it back. "I think you should try to get a good night's sleep now. Perhaps we will hear from her in the morning."

Ben got to his feet. "Yes, that's a good idea. I'm glad you came over Adam, tomorrow we will decide what to do. I can't think anymore for now, I need sleep." He patted Adam on the shoulder and looking as if he were sleep walking, left the room heading for his bed.

Adam let himself out of the house and headed for home.

The next morning Ben had a letter from Laura.

Darling Daddy,

Sorry I left so abruptly but I need to be on my own for a while. As you know, Adam and I have been seeing quite a lot of each other. I now feel I have been caught up in circumstances that are moving just too fast. I know this seems the coward's way out but I feel it's better for everyone this way.

If Adam calls will you tell him I think we were carried away with the idea of being in love. We should each go our own way.

Please don't worry about me. I am having a great time. Richard and Jane are spoiling me rotten. Forgive me for running off. I will phone you soon.

Love and miss you lots

Laura

Ben had just finished reading the letter when Adam arrived at the front door. He looked as if he hadn't had any sleep. Ben took him into the kitchen and sat him down.

"I was going to call you Adam, I have a letter from Laura." He saw Adam's eyes light up as he handed him the letter.

Adam's face turned white as he read it. Without a word he handed the letter back to Ben and walked out.

Ben watched him leave and for the only time in his life felt angry with his daughter.

Adam got into his car and sat staring into space. He couldn't believe Laura would do that to him. They were in love, they were happy. Something must have happened. He went over and over in his mind all of the conversations they had had the last days they were together. There were only good times. There was nothing to justify Laura running away like she had. Adam became angry. How dare she behave like this? To leave without a word was unforgivable. What a fool he felt. He would have given her everything but she chose to throw it all in his face. Well she could go to hell.

He turned the key in the ignition and took off as if all the furies of hell were behind him.

He spent the rest of the day alternating between feeling heartbroken and furious. He wanted to fly out to Laura and beg her to return, he wanted to shake some sense into her. He wanted the terrible pain to go away but if she didn't come back to him he knew it never would.

At dinner time that night he could only push his food around his plate.

Amanda noticed he was drinking more wine than he usually did. She imagined Laura had something to do with it. She couldn't help feeling afraid. What if Laura had decided to tell Adam about their little talk? Adam might go to confront his father. She was wondering if she had gone too far this time. She glanced at Tim and a feeling of panic came over her. She could never lose this man; she loved him so much.

Adam suddenly pushed his chair back and stood up. "Mother, Father, I have something to tell you. It seems I won't be getting married now. For reasons best know to Laura, she had decided to end our relationship altogether. I don't want to talk about it now or at any other time. Now if you will excuse me I would like an early night." He kissed his mother on the cheek and left.

Amanda was jubilant. She didn't think it would be so easy. She closed her eyes and bit her bottom lip. Tears of relief rolled down her cheeks.

Tim put down his napkin and went over to Amanda. "Hush darling don't cry. Things will be alright, wait and see." He gently pulled Amanda out of her chair and held her tenderly, mistaking her tears of relief as compassion for their son.

Amanda put her arms around her husband's neck and felt safer than she had in ages. A smile of triumph lit up her face.

Upstairs, Adam stood looking out of the window. It was one thing putting on an act for his parents but he could never fool himself. He felt his whole world had fallen apart. The anger that had overwhelmed him before had died, leaving him desolate. He leaned his forehead onto the cool glass of the window and stared out into the garden.

The sun was almost gone. Fantastic colours blazed across the sky. From deepest orange to pale gold, dark sandy coloured clouds drifted away on the last breath of wind. Adam thought how Laura might paint such a sunset. With a groan he banged his head on the glass. Would he ever be able to forget her? Did she really want to give up what they had? He couldn't believe she would end it. How could he be expected to get on with his life as if he had never known her? He stood at the window long after the sun had gone. His mind going over everything Laura and he had done, trying to find a clue to make some sense out of this nightmare.

After a while he became aware of being cold. The moon was shining down into the garden, he hadn't noticed the night stealing into this desolate world. He looked up at the stars and wondered if Laura would somehow feel his pain or the love that he sent out to her, soaring up into the vastness of the universe.

"If you ever loved me," he whispered, "feel me now."

Chapter Twenty-One

Ben was sitting in his favourite armchair, enjoying a glass of brandy. He had thought about going out but he really didn't have the heart. As usual he was thinking about Laura. The house was so empty now. He was toying with the idea of flying out to South Africa to see her. Maybe he could persuade her to come home now. In fact he would give her a ring right now, after all there was no point in sitting here alone worrying about her when he could be with her in a few hours.

He swallowed the last of his drink and reached for the telephone. As he lifted it to his ear the doorbell rang. Swearing to himself under his breath he went to open the door. At first he didn't recognise the person standing there. She was dressed in a bright pink outfit that was so tight she must have a problem walking. On the top of her so obviously bleached hair was perched a hat that to Ben looked like an abandoned birds nest. She was shifting her weight from one foot to the other as if she didn't know whether to run away or not.

Looking Ben in his eyes she smiled and said, "Long time no see Ben."

Ben's jaw dropped open. She was the last person in the world he expected to see. He stood speechless, his brain racing back to the past.

"Eve," he said at last. "What on earth brings you here?"

"Are you going to invite me in then?" she asked, giving him a nervous smile.

Ben opened the door wide and stepped back. "Sorry, come in." He led the way to the sitting room and indicated a chair.

She sat down and looked slowly around the room taking in everything. She was clearly impressed by what she saw. "You did alright for yourself Ben. All this time I felt guilty about leaving you and the little un and here you are in the lap of luxury."

Ben didn't know how to react, part of him was angry but there was a part of him that was glad to see her, even after all this time. Then it was as if a dam had burst and he was shouting at her, wanting to hurt her for leaving a helpless baby and humiliating him. Well he had managed very well without her, yes and Laura had also. He towered above Eve as he vented all of the frustrations of the last few months onto her.

It wasn't so much anger at his wife, to be honest he'd gotten over her pretty quickly. It was a chance to let go. He had needed somebody to shout at and now he did so.

"You might see it as luxury Eve but I see it as a reward for years of bloody hard work. Years of struggling to raise our daughter alone after you went swanning off with your fancy man. Did you ever wonder how we were? Did you ever think of your daughter on her first day at school or her first date? I bet you never lost any sleep wondering about us. Well as you can see, we did very well without you. Looking at you I would say we did far better than you did. How is your fancy man by the way? Not keeping you in the style you would like to become accustomed to I imagine."

Eve had gone very white. She bent her head and Ben could see her shoulders shaking as she silently wept.

He didn't know how to deal with this situation. He took out his handkerchief and thrust it into her hand. Now he was feeling guilty. He walked over to the drinks cabinet and poured a very large gin and tonic for Eve and a stiff brandy for himself. He went to her and put the drink into her hand.

"I bet you still drink G and T."

She nodded and took the drink, sipped it and put it down.

Ben sat down opposite her and for the first time really looked at her. He saw a thin, middle-aged woman. The thick make-up could not hide the lines in her face. There were streaks of grey growing through her hair. On closer inspection, he could see her clothes were clean but shabby. All at once he felt sorry for her. She didn't look as if she had found the better life she had been looking for.

As if reading his thoughts, she sat back in her seat and looked him in the eyes. "I expect I asked for that Ben," she said. "The truth is I did think about Laura. More than I thought I would in fact. I don't expect you will believe this but I thought of you as well. There were times when I would have done anything to turn back the clock but I had burned my bridges good and proper. When I ran off with Frank I thought we were made for each other. I was mad about him then. We got ourselves a job on a cruise ship, working in a cocktail bar. For the first few weeks it was fine, then he got friendly with one of the waitresses. The first port we called at he jumped ship with her.

"I was left on my own. Serves me right I suppose. Anyway I got used to it and it wasn't that bad really. I stayed with the ship for a few years. It was good seeing a bit of the world. I even met a couple that came from these parts once. They were on Honeymoon. I wanted to ask if they knew you and Laura but I didn't in the end. Too ashamed I suppose. After a while I met another bloke and he was good to me. He was American. I gave up work and moved in with him. He was a really nice bloke Ben. We were happy for a while. I even got pregnant again."

She stopped talking, lowered her eyes and burst into tears again.

Ben sat in silence. Should he go and comfort her?" There was no need. Eve stopped crying, blew her nose and in a much smaller voice continued.

"I had a little girl. She was so beautiful Ben. All at once it was as if I was being given another chance to make up for leaving Laura. This time around I was ready to be a mother. I wanted to be the best mum ever. I was too, for a little while."

Now the tears were rolling down her cheeks again as she continued.

"We were so happy Ben. I know I didn't deserve it but everything had worked out just fine. Then one day we were on the way home from shopping. It was dark and raining cats and dogs. There were these two kids, only about fifteen, They had stolen a car and were trying to get away from the police. They swerved right in front of us and we hit head on. Poor Steve was driving; there wasn't a thing he could do to avoid the car. It happened so quickly. One minute we were as happy as larry, the next my world came to an end. Steve was killed outright. My beautiful girl died in the ambulance."

Ben leaned over and took her hands in his. He didn't say anything; he just let her cry. Instinctively he knew she was crying out the pain that had been locked inside her. In some strange way he knew he was the only person she could allow herself to be natural with. She had let her defences down knowing that after all she had done to him, or maybe because of it, he would be a comfort to her.

He thought about Laura and how much she meant to him. How could he bear it if anything happened to her? Poor Eve, she had lost everything in the space of a few minutes.

After a while her crying stopped. She gave Ben a sad little smile.

"That's the first time I've cried in years you know. Sorry Ben, I didn't mean to."

Ben stood up and pulled her to her feet. "Don't be sorry Eve, you needed to. Now would you take it the wrong way if I said you needed a cuddle?"

Her face was transformed into the biggest smile. "Oh Ben please."

They stood there for some time just holding each other. Both needed the comfort of a shoulder to lean on. Ben could feel how thin she was. All the anger he felt earlier seemed to evaporate, time had moved on and Eve had suffered in a way that he could never imagine. He wanted to protect her. There was no point in thinking about the past now. Both of them had made mistakes, they had been too young to marry. With a shock Ben realised they were still married. It seemed strange to think this woman was still his wife. Gently he released her.

"I think we could both do with another drink."

Eve smiled and passed her glass. "You always did know what was good for me."

Ben poured the drinks and they carried on talking. It grew dark and he switched on the lights. Now both were relaxed and the soft glow made Eve look younger. The haunted look she had when she arrived had disappeared.

Ben realised he was starving. Looking at his watch he was amazed to see it was well after twelve. "I didn't realise it was so late. I'm hungry, how about you?"

Eve nodded. "Now you mention it, I could eat a horse."

Ben grinned. "No horse, but I do a mean steak and chips as long as you peel the potatoes."

Eve stood up. "Just point me in the direction of the kitchen. I might even wash up as well."

After they had enjoyed their meal and put the dishes in the dishwasher, they sat drinking coffee in the kitchen. Both were now relaxed with each other.

Ben gave an enormous yawn and stood up. "I think it's time we thought about bed. Don't worry, there are plenty of rooms upstairs. You can take your pick. You can't go anywhere at this time of night so you may as well get your head down."

Eve slowly stood up. "Ben you're a life saver. I can hardly keep my eyes open. I didn't expect us to get on like this." Her eyes filled with tears and Ben put his arm around her shoulder.

"None of that now. I reckon we both need a good night's sleep. Off you go then." He gave her a peck on the cheek and turned her towards the door. "It's only one night, no big deal. Just don't expect me to bring you breakfast in bed."

In fact, it turned out to be much more than one night.

They started talking over breakfast and by the evening they were finding out more and more about each other, each saying things they had never imagined possible to share.

The result was that Eve stayed another night, then another. At the end of a week Ben found he was actually singing to his reflection in the mirror as he was shaving. With a shock he realised it had been days since he had thought about Laura. In fact, he hadn't been this happy in years. He decided he would take Eve out for a special meal that evening. There was something he wanted to ask her.

Ben had chosen a quiet restaurant that served excellent food. They were relaxing over coffee when Ben took Eve by the hand. He looked into her face, noticing how the gaunt look she had when she first arrived had gone.

He coughed nervously. "Eve I know this may come as a bit of a surprise to you but I need you to know I have been so happy since you came back into my life. Could you ever consider moving back in with me? I think we have more going for us now than when we were a couple of kids still wet behind the ears."

Eve looked at Ben and there were tears in her eyes. "Oh Ben, I don't know what to say. I didn't think you could ever forgive me for walking out on you and Laura, are you sure you want this?"

Ben squeezed her fingers. "It's not that silly young girl I want back, it's the woman she's become."

This was too much for Eve. She burst into tears. Ignoring the looks they were getting from other diners, Ben went to Eve and pulled her into his arms.

"Hey it's not that bad an idea is it?"

Smiling through her tears, Eve looked into Ben's eyes and feeling as if she could burst with happiness, she could only whisper, "Yes please Ben."

Chapter Twenty-Two

Ben had never been happier in his life. He was sitting with Eve drinking champagne. That afternoon they had once again made their wedding vows to each other.

Side by side they said words that had come from the heart. This time it would be for keeps.

Eve had blossomed since they had been together again. She had put on a few pounds, losing that gaunt look. Her hair was back to its original colour. True, there were a few grey strands but Ben loved them. He said they both were officially grown up at last and their hair colour was proof of their new status in life.

He had delighted in buying Eve a new wardrobe and showing her off. Introducing her to all of his friends and if anyone showed surprise Ben would laugh and say they couldn't be more surprised than he was himself.

As each week passed they grew closer than they ever dreamed possible. At first, they would talk for hours. Then as time went on they found contentment in just being together in companionable silence. Each lost in their own thoughts of wonder how things could change so dramatically in life. They were two different people from when they first married. The love they now shared was deeper, unselfish and for the first time trusting.

Ben put his drink down and standing up reached down to pull Eve up and into his arms. He lifted her hand with the new wedding ring shining on her finger and kissed it. The look on her face made words unnecessary.

"Well Mrs Woods, I think now is the time to spring a little surprise on you. I left it till the last minute because I know you will be nervous about it. I told you all about Laura and her problems, what I didn't tell you is I phoned Laura and told her all about us. She was delighted with the news and insisted we both go out to see her. She said she wanted to come home to see me last month but there was a reason she couldn't travel and that she had an even bigger surprise for us so we should go as soon as possible. The surprise is there is a flight leaving to Cape Town at eight in the morning and we are booked on it so we had better get packing."

Eve looked totally shocked and then burst into tears.

Ben was terrified he'd got it wrong. Stroking her hair he held her to him wondering what he should do now. Gradually Eve stopped crying. Ben gave her a handkerchief and she blew her nose. He pulled her back down on the sofa and cuddled her.

"I'm sorry darling; we don't have to go if you don't want to. I'll ring Laura and tell her we won't be going."

Eve gave a shaky laugh. "Don't you dare. I can't wait to see my daughter again. I never dreamed I would get the chance."

Ben's face lit up. "But I thought... when you cried..."

Eve cupped his face with her hands. "That's what some women do when they're happy you wonderful man and I am so happy."

Ben gave a sigh of complete satisfaction. "I'm very glad to hear it 'cos that makes two of us. Now I think we had better start getting organised. We have a plane to catch but the way I feel right now I could fly without one."

Eve gave a giggle. "and I'm very glad to hear it 'cos that makes two of us."

*****

Laura couldn't sleep. She could hardly take in the news her father had told her on the phone. Imagine her mother back with her father. Her mother, she couldn't even remember her. How could it be her mother, hadn't Mrs Knight told her who her real mother was? What if she had been lying? Maybe she hadn't wanted Adam to marry her so she had made up this story to prevent it. Surely that just couldn't be true. What if it was?

She was dizzy thinking about it. All would become clear when she saw her beloved Daddy again. She had missed him so much. It seemed they had been separated for years. He would make everything right; she should have gone to him in the first place instead of running away. It was a complete bombshell about her mother but she had no doubt her father was going to feel the same when he met his new granddaughter. She was so beautiful. When she had been born six weeks ago, Laura had been overwhelmed. The baby looked so much like Adam her heart felt as if it would break all over again.

At the sound of the first whimper, Laura was out of bed before the baby could start a full blown cry. She didn't want Richard and Jane to wake up. She could never repay them for the care and love they repeatedly gave her. Tenderly she picked up her baby. She sat by the window rocking her in her arms while gazing at the starlit sky. Now Laura didn't feel the mind numbing ache of loneliness. She could look up and feel at peace. She could imagine the heavens a big velvety blanket with stars woven amongst it and she had it draped over her and her baby in their own oasis of peace. She looked at her sleeping child, in a few hours she would meet her granddad.

*****

"There she is! There's our girl." Ben had spotted her instantly. That wonderful hair shone out like sunshine after a storm. The next minute Laura was swept up in a bear hug. She buried her face into him and as the tears fell down her cheeks she breathed in his dear familiar smell and was once again his little girl.

Eve stood watching. Part of her wanted to turn and run, the other part wanted to belong to Laura as much as Ben. She could only stand and wait. She felt she had no right to expect anything from Laura and she certainly didn't deserve anything. For what seemed hours she stood watching her husband and daughter.

Ben released Laura at last. Putting his hands on her shoulders he smiled down at her and turning her gently towards Eve said, "I have someone here who's been longing to see you again sweetheart."

Eve held her breath. She couldn't speak. She was looking into a pair of green eyes that were swimming with tears and she was powerless to tear hers away. The world stopped. She had no idea what to do. Fear of rejection had frozen her. She waited for the insults to start pouring over her. She longed for them to start now, hurry and get it over with. She should have stayed away. There was no room for her here. She must catch the next flight home and walk out of their lives once again.

Laura lifted her hand and touched Eve tentatively on the arm. It had the effect of a bolt of lightning. With a cry that sounded like a wounded animal, Eve pulled Laura into her arms and rocked her like a baby.

Laura hadn't known how she would react or what she would feel at this meeting and was totally shocked at her own reaction. She wanted to hold on to this woman. It felt right. She had thought she was fine without her in her life. Now she knew she had always needed her and the shock was overwhelming.

Ben stood watching the two people he loved most in the world. He wasn't aware of the tears pouring down his face. Around them people were scurrying with bags, struggling with fractious children and going about their normal lives. A trolley pushed into Ben's ankle, which brought him down to earth. Vigorously blowing his nose then putting his handkerchief away he quietly guided the two women to a coffee bar, although he would have much preferred something stronger.

Seated with cups of hot coffee in front of them, the talking began.

Hours later they were still talking. Sitting in Richard and Jane's garden in the cool of the evening the average observer would have thought it an idyllic scene. Nobody could have guessed revelations just exchanged would bring about such changes in the lives of the people gathered there.

Ben couldn't believe he was a grandfather. When he had gotten over the shock, he had fallen instantly in love with the tiny girl. The icing on the cake for him was when Laura told him she was going to name the baby Jenny.

He was shocked to the core when Laura had told him everything Amanda Knight had said. Richard was afraid he was going to have a heart attack at one stage. Ben had gone deathly white and was shaking so much he had to lie down. He couldn't believe the wicked lies and the suffering that woman had put Laura and himself through, not to mention her own son. What did she have to gain by spewing out such poison?

He intended to get to the bottom of it as soon as he returned home. In the meantime, there was at least one thing he could do to undo some of the damage that had been done to his beloved daughter. He had lost no time in putting his plan into action. The only one that had no idea about it was Laura but before too long, with luck, she would.

A hand on Ben's arm brought him back to the present. Richard was pointing over to Eve. Exhausted with jet lag and the events of the day, she had fallen asleep in her chair.

"Well folks," Ben said, "I reckon someone is all talked out for now. If you will excuse us I think we had better say goodnight. I don't think there will ever be another day quite like this ever again." He walked over to Jane and kissed her on both cheeks. Turning to Laura he pulled her up and into his arms. "As for you miss, I will see you in the morning."

Tenderly he woke his sleeping wife who was mortified for having falling asleep. Ten minutes later she had fallen into bed and into an ever deeper sleep.

Laura lay in her bed thinking over the events of the day. It was amazing what could happen in a few short hours. Was there such a thing as fate? Did destiny have everything mapped out from the minute you were born or did you have to seize your chances in life? Maybe it was her destiny to bring up her daughter without a father. If it was then she would see Jenny wanted for nothing. No child would ever be more loved.

She stared at the moonlight intruding into her room. As for herself, it was wonderful to have her father back again, her mother too, yes she was loved but oh how she wanted her real love as she had never wanted him before. Why then had the fates decided to steal that love from her forever?

Chapter Twenty-Three

The next morning Laura woke up very late. Jumping out of bed, she threw on her dressing gown and ran downstairs. There was a note on the table with her name on it. It was from her father saying they had all gone out for the day. They hadn't wanted to disturb her and they had taken the baby with them to give her a rest. Laura felt very disappointed and hurt about being left out. She wondered if she would be second best now her parents were together again. She didn't want to feel jealous but couldn't help feeling alone again. More alone in fact because she had thought she belonged to a family again. Blinking back tears she walked slowly upstairs.

An hour later she was still feeling miserable. What should she do to fill her time until the others were home. It was lonely without Jenny and she missed her baby.

Deciding to go and read in the garden, Laura was just going to find a book when the doorbell rang. Frowning, Laura went to open the door. At first she thought she was mistaken. Surely the sun was in her eyes, it couldn't be him. She shielded her eyes from the sun and looked again. Laura felt the world spinning and would have fallen had not Adam caught her in his arms. She could hear him murmuring words of love and feel his lips covering her face with kisses. Her eyes were closed and she dare not open them. This must be a dream but it felt so wonderful, so real she didn't want to wake up and feel that emptiness again. At last, Adam stood her on her feet and held her at arms length. Finally, Laura opened her eyes and gazed into that beloved face she thought she would never see again. That was her undoing. As if a dam had burst she started to cry.

All the months of pain, worry and suffering burst from her and she was totally unable to stop the outpouring of her grief.

Adam held her close to him, knowing it would do no good to try to stop her, she needed to cleanse herself of her past misery.

When at last she was able to speak, Laura had a thousand questions for him. What was Adam doing here? How did he know where to find her? Why had he come now?

Adam explained that Ben had telephoned him and told him to get over as soon as he could. Adam had needed no second telling and had hastily thrown some things into a bag and caught the next plane out without even leaving a note to explain his absence.

Now he was here he wanted an explanation from Laura. How could she had left without a word?

Laura decided to tell him everything. She would not spare his mother.

Adam was stunned when he discovered the real reason for Laura's leaving. He was filled with a cold fury. If his mother had been in the room he might have struck her, such was his anger. When he heard the news he was a father, Adam broke down and wept. He was thrilled at the news but the thought of his beloved Laura going through it all on her own when they should have been together, broke his heart. They had been cheated of this most precious time and he would never forgive his mother for it as long as he lived; still, now was not the moment to think of his mother. At last he was reunited with his beloved Laura and soon he would meet his baby daughter, things couldn't get any better.

It seemed no time at all before the others arrived home. Everyone started talking at once and the house was filled with noise, joy and love. Each one thought they were the happiest person alive but there was one who was sure now that after years of heartache the one thing missing in life was about to become real, but for now it was enough to bask in the feelings that radiated the house like liquid sunshine.

It was four weeks later, Jane and Richard were sitting in the garden enjoying the sounds and smells of evening. Laura and Adam had been married that day and were happily ensconced in their honeymoon hotel. They had entrusted their baby to the proud grandparents and now all three of them were on their way home. After the honeymoon the happy couple would be flying home and staying with Laura's parents while they looked for their dream home.

Richard gave a deep sigh. "Well my love it's been a hectic few weeks and I for one am not sorry to have our home back to ourselves again. I love them all dearly but I do like just being on our own together."

Jane stood up and held her hands out to Richard, gently she

pulled him up. "You had better make the most of it then because I can tell you it won't last."

Richard groaned and rested his head on his wife's shoulder. "Oh no, now who's coming?"

Jane smiled. "I won't be able to tell you for at least six months; unless you really want to know then I will have another scan and see if it's a boy or a girl." She looked up into his face to see a dozen emotions chasing each other.

Finally he could speak but he didn't make much sense. "Oh Jane... oh Jane... What... you mean... are you... are we... no you can't... it is really... Oh my love." Gathering her up in his arms he gave a whoop of pure joy and danced her around the garden.

Everything was now complete.

Chapter Twenty-Four

Amanda quietly pushed open the bedroom door. Tim was awake so she put down his cup of coffee and sat on the edge of the bed. He was looking very tired and pale. Amanda had been awake most of the night herself. Tim had been tossing and turning until the early hours. He pulled himself up and ran a hand through his hair before picking up his steaming coffee. Amanda went to the window and drew back the curtains.

"It's a beautiful day darling, we should make the most of it and spend time in the garden, the fresh air will do you good."

"Don't talk to me as if I were a child Amanda," Tim snapped. "I am quite able to decide what is or isn't good for me. May I drink my coffee in peace now please?"

Amanda was taken aback by this little outburst. She stood looking at him for a second then turned and left the room without a word.

Downstairs in the kitchen she sat nursing her own coffee unaware and uncaring that it was getting as cold as the look on her face. That little scene upstairs was not the first they had had lately by any means. Tim had such a short fuse these days. Amanda was getting more and more worried, he was spending more time on his own, not even wanting to talk. He would sit for hours at the bedroom window just staring at the big cedar tree. Other times he would stand beneath it and gaze up into it. She wondered what was in his mind, did it have anything to do with the past?

Her hand went to the pocket of her trouser suit and felt the crisp hardness of the letter that had arrived this morning. It had been addressed to Tim but she had instantly recognised the handwriting and had torn it open.

She didn't know whether she was more hurt or angry after reading what Adam had written. Her initial reaction was blind fury. Adam was married and had a daughter. Worse, he had told his father the part Amanda had played, trying to separate him from Laura. Now he would soon be home but not to his old home, he would be staying at the home of his new wife for the time being.

Amanda had never been so worried in her life. She had no idea what she was going to do next. How long would it be before her whole world came crashing down around her. Tim would never forgive her, she was sure of that. What would she do if Tim read the contents of this letter? She must destroy it at once. Amanda found a pair of scissors and cut the letter into tiny pieces, she then put them into the sink and set fire to them. Still feeling panicky she paced up and down; what was she to do next. She must play for time, yes that's it. She would go up to him now and suggest they go away today. Anywhere, right now. She would tell him they both needed a holiday and should go away right now, today, there was no reason why not. Amanda took a deep breath. She must stay calm, if she started to panic now she would lose everything. Stay calm she told herself and she would find a way out of this nightmare.

After all these years with Tim she wasn't going to let the shadow of that common little shop girl destroy her and her family.

Feeling more like her old self, Amanda went to see what Tim was doing. As she entered the bedroom she saw Tim was showered and dressed. He turned to her with a smile on his face.

"Sorry about earlier darling, I had a bad headache but I shouldn't have taken it out on you."

Amanda went to him and put her arms around his waist. "I understand dear but you have been getting a lot of them these days. I worry about you; in fact I've been thinking we could both do with a change of scene so I suggest we take a short holiday. Somewhere we haven't been before, what do you think?"

Tim smiled at her. "I think you usually get your own way so why not. Decide where you want to go and let's do it. Tell you what, let's go to a travel agent for some ideas, then we can find a nice pub and have lunch. I feel like spoiling you today."

Amanda was thrilled. It had been so easy. Feeling in control again she gave him a squeeze. "What did I do to deserve you? Give me five minutes and I will be all yours."

Three hours later they were sitting at a table to the side of a big inglenook fireplace. There was a log burning fire giving off a beautiful smell of apple wood. The flames from the fire reflected and danced over copper jugs and pans hanging over and around the fire.

Amanda was enchanted with it. The smile on her lips faded as she saw the expression on Tim's face.

When they had walked into the pub, Tim had gone immediately to the table they were sitting at. It was as if he were very familiar with this place, it seemed to welcome him like an old friend. He had a feeling of great joy when he had looked into the flames of the fire. The colours were hypnotic, he couldn't look away. He felt the old familiar pain beginning at his temples, knowing that soon it would crush him and blot out... what? Now the feeling of happiness had gone and still he couldn't look away from the fire. The colours leaped and twirled changing all the time. The reflections on the copper looked almost like the colour of her wonderful hair. Whose hair? Where had that thought come from? Who was 'she'?

The image of the woman who had haunted him over the years was there but again he couldn't see her face. Never could he see her face but always the feeling of despair and longing. Why did he feel his life was incomplete? The pain was getting stronger and Tim knew there would be no respite for hours yet.

Amanda knew the carefree day they were enjoying was over. Looking at Tim she knew he needed to be home. Gently she covered his hands with her. "Darling I think we had better get you home."

Tim jumped at the sound of her voice.

She looked into his eyes and saw infinite sadness and knew once again that he was going back into himself to a place where she couldn't reach him. Back were her old feelings of turmoil and fear. Would there ever be a time when she could live in peace with her husband? Perhaps she should think about living abroad. If she could get Tim to consider it maybe her troubles would be over. The more she thought about it the more she warmed to the idea. A new start in a new country maybe the answer.

It wasn't until they were almost home that Amanda realised they hadn't eaten lunch. Tim didn't want anything to eat so Amanda went upstairs with him and drew the curtain while Tim lay down. She went into the bathroom and ran a towel under the cold tap. Returning to his beside she gently soothed his forehead.

He reached up and caught her hand. "Please leave me Amanda, I'll be fine soon."

She kissed him gently. "You rest now Tim, I'll pop back later." She tiptoed out of the room and closed the door quietly behind her.

What she wanted now was coffee, a sandwich and time to plan their future. If the future didn't include their only son then so be it. Still, she would find a way to make Laura pay for ever marrying her beloved boy. No relative of Jenny Woods would get the better of her.

Amanda woke up with a start. She hadn't realised she had fallen asleep. She must have been more tired than she thought, after all she'd had a terrible night last night. It had grown dark and there was a full moon. Amanda drew the curtains then remembering Tim was still lying down, ran lightly up the stairs.

He was still asleep but at some time he had woken up and put on the bedside light, now he was propped up on his pillows. Amanda stood looking down at him. She still loved him with all her heart. She went to the window to draw the curtain, just as she was reaching out Tim cried out. His voice so loud and unexpected, Amanda jumped.

Startled she turned to him; he looked at her and held out his arms. His eyes were wide open and there was an expression on his face she had never seen before. It was pure love. Her heart skipped a beat as he threw back the covers and took a step towards her.

"Oh my love it's really you. You're here at last, oh my darling my sweet sweet darling."

Horror swept through Amanda as she realised Tim wasn't looking at her but over her shoulder. She felt her blood turn to ice crystals and knew for certain that Tim wasn't talking to her. The truth hit her but she wouldn't believe it. As if to reinforce her most hideous nightmare, Tim carried on talking and she was powerless to move or speak.

Her head was spinning and she wanted to be sick but she was transfixed. Somehow her legs were holding her up. She wanted to blot out what she was seeing and hearing but her tortured mind would not give her that relief. His next words were more than she could bear and she gave a moan like a wounded animal, while inside, her heart died.

"Oh Jenny my darling I can see you now. It was you, all these years you were there in my mind and now I have you again. Forever my love, forever."

Tim took one more step and fell.

Amanda knew he was dead. Unable to move, she stood in a daze staring down at the only man she had ever loved. She had stolen him from another woman and made him live a lie but she would do it all over again if she could.

She turned and walked over to the window. Resting her head on the cold glass she looked down into the moonlit garden. A movement under the big old cedar tree caught her eye, a shadow within a shadow.

Amanda thought nothing could hurt her anymore, she was wrong.

As she watched in disbelief she saw Jenny and Tim with their arms around each other, dressed as they had been on the night of their engagement. She saw Tim gently stroke Jenny's hair and an echo of tinkling laughter floated into the room.

Before they finally faded away, Amanda saw a brilliant flash of a diamond on Jenny's finger. Then Amanda knew she was alone forever.

She had lost.